WE'VE ALREADY
GONE THIS FAR

WE'VE ALREADY GONE THIS FAR

PATRICK DACEY

HENRY HOLT AND COMPANY

NEW YORK

Henry Holt and Company, LLC
Publishers since 1866
175 Fifth Avenue
New York, New York 10010
www.henryholt.com

Some of these stories have appeared elsewhere in slightly different form:
"Patriots" in *Bomb* magazine, #104, Summer 2008; "The Place You
Are Going To" in *Sou'wester*, Fall 2010; "Lost Dog" in *Zoetrope: All-Story*,
vol. 17, no. 1, Spring 2013; "Never So Sweet" as "Departures" in *Guernica*,
May 2013; "Incoming Mail" in *Lumina*, vol. XIII, 2014; "Downhill"
in *Barrelhouse*, issue 13, Winter 2014; "Ballad" in *Cleaver*, issue 6,
Winter 2014 and in *Mission at Tenth*, vol. 5, Summer 2014; "To Feel Again the
Kind of Love That Hurts Something Terrible" as "Love, Women" in *The Paris
Review* No. 214, Fall 2015.

Library of Congress Cataloging-in-Publication Data

Dacey, Patrick.
  [Short stories. Selections]
  We've already gone this far / Patrick Dacey. — First edition.
     pages cm
  ISBN 978-1-62779-465-7 (hardcover) — ISBN 978-1-62779-466-4 (ebook)
  I. Title.
  PS3604.A215
  [A6 2015]
  813'.6—dc23

                                                    2015003308

Henry Holt books are available for special promotions and premiums.
For details contact: Director, Special Markets.

First Edition 2016

Designed by Meryl Sussman Levavi

Printed in the United States of America

1   3   5   7   9   10   8   6   4   2

For my son, Colin Archer Dacey

The strangeness of life, the more you resisted it, the harder it bore down on you. The more the mind opposed the sense of strangeness, the more distortions it produced. What if, for once, one were to yield to it?

—SAUL BELLOW

CONTENTS

~~~

WE'VE ALREADY
GONE THIS FAR

PATRIOTS

～～～

DURING THE WAR, most of us in Wequaquet hung up a flag to support the troops, though it was clear some of us did it because others were doing it. We pulled out our flags from the last war or went to Hal's and bought a new one. Hal sold out pretty fast, and good for Hal, because usually no one goes to Hal's anymore, the way he charges, though he says he has no choice if he wants to compete with MegaWorld.

Donna Baker went the extra mile. I didn't mind the oversize flag snapping in the wind from the holder beside her door so much as I minded having to look across the street at all the little flags stuck in the lawn and in the light holders on the garage and on the antenna of her Subaru.

After a strong wind or rain, I'd see her out there picking up those little flags and then pushing them back in the dirt or snow and packing the dirt or snow around the little sticks. I would watch her do this while I had my breakfast, and, I'll admit, I timed my breakfast for when she did this.

Then one day, when I saw Donna driving off in her stupid Subaru, I went right across the street and took one of the flags out of the ground and buried it in my backyard. I don't know why. I respected her patriotic pride. Really, I did. Her son, Justin, was over there, and that must've been hard, but no harder than your son fixing city bridges or removing asbestos or driving a stock car. Actually, the most dangerous job in the world is cutting timber. I looked it up. And when Donna got back, she was carrying a bag of groceries in her arms, looking over the flags in her yard, counting each and every one of them. She put down her groceries and stood there for a half hour, counting and recounting and scratching her head. She went next door to the Putters' house, but I guess she forgot they both have jobs and no one would be home. He teaches history at the high school and she's a hairstylist—actually a haircutter. She works at Uppercuts, and what they did to my hair once was not styling.

Then Donna Baker walked across the street to my house and knocked on the door. I didn't answer. Then I heard her knocking on my back sliding door. She was standing on my porch and we saw each other and I made like I was cleaning up some mess behind the couch and gave her the "I'll be there in a second" finger. Then I let her in. She said, "You think those hoodlums are back?" and I thought, the last time we had hoodlums was when her son and a couple of his friends ripped out every mailbox on our street and tore down street signs and stole doghouses and dismantled a billboard and spray-painted WELCOME TO FUCK WORLD on it and put it in Barry Park and that Sunday kids were all asking their parents, "What's Fuck World?" and I thought to say we haven't had any criminal activity around here since your son, you know, but I didn't, and I shrugged and said, "Would you like some coffee, Donna?"

We talked for a while. She was upset about the new standardized testing at the schools and I mentioned a movie I wanted to see that she hadn't seen, either, and so we made a casual plan to go see it but never did. And then she said, "You know, if I had to do it all over again, I'd live close to the water," and I agreed. Then she left and drove off in her Subaru and came back later with another little flag and put it right in the same spot where I'd taken her other one.

I KNOW some things about Donna Baker. People talk. For instance, I know that her sister has a drug habit and stole all her jewelry and took off to Utah, and I thought, Utah? I also know that Donna drives down to the new development in Spring Creek just to watch the men work. I know she's put on twenty pounds—anyone can see that, but not anyone can see that she sneaks mini-muffins in her car every morning. I also know that she drives twenty miles out to Wareham and sings karaoke at Tenderhearts, because my cousin is a bartender there. He says Donna Baker's a terrible singer.

I'm sure she knows some things about me, too.

She knows, like everyone knows, that my husband ran out on me less than a year ago after they shot a movie here in town and he got a bit part as a short-order cook at a diner with his line "Flapjacks and bacon," which he practiced day and night in the house. The lead, a detective, asks a waitress at the counter for flapjacks and bacon, then the waitress says, "Flapjacks and bacon," and Paul repeats, "Flapjacks and bacon."

They didn't even use his line in the movie. But Paul was passionate. He said it didn't matter how old he was, he was going out to Hollywood to try his hand at it, and if he didn't try his hand at it, then he'd resent himself for the rest of his life and he'd die an angry man. I'll tell you this. If my husband were shot dead, more people would've come over and said how sorry they were.

WHEN JUSTIN left, Donna Baker stuck a dozen or so yellow-ribbon stickers to the back and sides of her Subaru. We all know the yellow-ribbon sticker is there to support the troops, and who wouldn't? But I'll bet Donna doesn't know that the yellow-ribbon sticker is also a symbol for suicide prevention, bone cancer, and endometriosis. It's true. I looked it up. After Justin died, Donna took down the yellow-ribbon stickers and stuck a white-ribbon sticker to the bumper of her Subaru. It's a symbol of innocence. It represents victims of terrorism. It's also a symbol for retinoblastoma, which makes sense. But it's black from the mud and dirty snow and you can't clean a ribbon sticker, and a black-ribbon sticker is a symbol for gang prevention, which I know Donna Baker supports, too, after all, but I don't think she knows that's what it means now.

JUSTIN'S WELCOME-HOME party was not fun like parties should be, like the party Gail Prager threw for her father-in-law when he turned eighty-two. Being around someone that old made you feel good to be where you were in life; it made you feel like you had time left. There was a cake, but Mr. Prager couldn't eat the cake, because he couldn't open his mouth wide enough to take in food, and when Gail's daughter, Francesca, tried to feed him the cake, she ended up just smearing it over Mr. Prager's lips and cheeks, and we all laughed.

That was a feel-good party. It didn't even matter that they were Jewish.

Hard to feel good when someone comes back from a war.

You see it on television and you figure the one you know is the one hollering and firing his automatic weapon into the dunes, and, really, how do you react to someone like that?

There wasn't any cake. There wasn't even music. What kind of party doesn't have cake and music? Justin brought a woman with him, Kiki-something. Who names their daughter Kiki? I mean, you might as well set up one of those stripper poles in her bedroom, right? She was so tall, almost another body taller than me. She had a big, round chin and wore gaudy makeup and was dressed in this leopard-print sundress, and we all figured she was a whore. She ate more than anyone at the party. Justin was sitting on a beach chair on the back lawn, rolling cigarettes and smoking and sipping a beer, and some people walked around him and others stood near him and a few shook his hand and asked him questions. His super-tall woman sat down on his lap and at one point I saw them necking and it looked like she was eating him. Calvin Baker grilled hamburgers and hot dogs and brats, because that's Justin's favorite, but Justin didn't eat one and the brats were piled up on a serving plate that Donna Baker gave to George Falachi because the Falachis are poor and she felt bad for them, which I'll tell you is in poor and bad taste to do in front of people at a party.

The main reason why it wasn't a good party for me was because later, after a few too many gin and tonics and Jimmy Buffett songs, Donna Baker and I got into an argument about the war. She was saying how we were doing great things over there, building schools, establishing a government, letting the people decide what's best for their country, et cetera. And I interrupted, saying how I thought that was all political propaganda, that we couldn't even get that right in *this* fucking country, how were we going to get it right over there? Right? And she called me a traitor, and I called her a gullible bitch, and she said I was a condescending wacko, and I said she was an unrealistic cunt, and she said that my collection of wind chimes drives her nuts, and I said her collection of flags and ribbons drives *me* nuts, and she said that the brownies I brought over were dry and you could see nobody wanted them, and I said her potato salad tasted like fucking glue. Then she called for Justin, and everyone stopped and stared at him. Donna Baker said, "Tell her, Justin. Go ahead." And Justin said, "Tell her what?" and Donna Baker said, "Tell her what it's like," and Justin said, "It's like nothing." Then we sort of drifted back to our houses, trying not to upset all the little flags in the yard. Two weeks later, Justin went back, and Donna Baker kept up with her flags and ribbon stickers, and we didn't talk for a while.

THE SUMMER passed. I spent most of my time on the back porch. Sometimes I cried about Paul. Sometimes I broke a dish or a glass. One day Donna Baker came by to warn me that the terror level had been raised to red. I didn't know what that meant. She seemed pretty nervous.

"I doubt they'll come after any of us, Donna," I said.

"You can't be too sure. For my sake, keep your eyes peeled."

"Okay, Donna."

She warned everyone in the neighborhood, except for Muslim Joe, who I sometimes think might just be wearing that turban so no one bothers him.

After Labor Day, Nancy Dwyer came over with some gossip. She was all excited, like she gets when bad things happen to one of us, standing in the kitchen with her chest sticking out like two torpedoes that have taken off but won't ever land. She told me she saw Donna's husband, Calvin, out in Falmouth, having coffee with a gorgeous woman at Dunkin' Donuts. I don't know too many gorgeous women that drink coffee at Dunkin' Donuts, and Nancy's a big liar, anyway. (She once told Cindy Putter that the reason I didn't have kids was because I didn't like the way they looked. All kids, mind you. Of course, I don't like how some kids look. Some kids are real ugly. Kids like Cindy Putter's kids. The reason I didn't *have* kids is because I didn't *want* kids.) "They're going to split," she said, and she held her hand to her throat as if something were stuck in it. "Can you believe it?"

I thought, hearing that about Calvin, Donna might stop by to ask me what it was like to lose a husband, because, even though I didn't like a lot of things about her, she was still my neighbor. But she didn't stop by, and so I thought, You're on your own, Donna Baker.

Then I heard that Donna was setting up a committee to send parcels and gift boxes over to the soldiers to let them know that we cared over here. Those I had spoken to said they didn't RSVP because of how things turned out at the party. And even though I wasn't invited, I said I didn't RSVP, either. We all agreed that it was better we didn't have it right in our faces anymore. Most of us didn't keep up with the war, and because it was almost football season, our neighborhood was more concerned with what the Red Raiders were going to look like in the fall, rather than any new developments over there.

IN OCTOBER, Justin was killed by one of his own men. I found out from Nancy, who had read about it at the grocery, and I knew she was telling the truth because she was shivering and crying and she hugged me, and Nancy never hugs. After she told me, I spent the next couple of days looking across the street to see if Donna would come out and then maybe I'd act like I was leaving to get something at the store and could just bump into her and say how sorry I was about her son, because really I was.

But I didn't see her, not until that Saturday, when Calvin Baker showed up. And Donna came out crying and crying, and then Calvin tried to hug her, but Donna stepped away and doubled over, and even though we weren't on speaking terms, I couldn't stand seeing her cry, and I started crying. Then Calvin grabbed her from behind and pulled her into him, and I could see some of my neighbors looking out of their windows, and I figured they were thinking like I was. Thinking what it must've felt like to be Donna Baker just then.

THE FUNERAL was very sad. The biggest, toughest men you've ever seen broke down. Donna Baker took the folded flag and put it on her lap and she let Calvin hold her hand, which was sweet, considering. George Falachi wore sunglasses even though there wasn't any sun that day, and I guessed he was probably stoned. Nancy Dwyer asked me how much I paid for my bouquet at Jane's, and I told her too much. Gail Prager wasn't there and we all noticed that. Cindy Putter and her husband, Leonard, brought their two kids and they ran around the plots, jumping over the buried bones, taking the flags from the ground and playing swords with them.

When the soldiers raised their guns and fired, I flinched.

AFTER THE funeral, I decided to take my wind chimes down. I'm not sure why I started collecting them in the first place. I liked listening to them clatter and ring in uneven tones. It was a nice distraction in the morning and at night. I didn't think; I listened. It's good for me not to be thinking all the time.

As I was taking them down, I heard footsteps behind me and I turned and there was Donna Baker, and she said, "Why don't you leave a few up? I can hear them from across the street. They're pleasant at night."

I said, "Okay, Donna."

Then I felt good. I felt so good that the next day I planned on returning her little flag. I'd put down a bluestone over the hole where I buried the flag, and I'd uncovered the flag and picked up the bluestone to put it in the garage when I saw Donna Baker pushing a cross into her lawn. I thought, This is ridiculous, and really I was going to go over there and pull it right out, but the bluestone fell from my arms and landed on my foot.

WHEN WE got back from the hospital, Donna helped me inside. Then she ran to her house and grabbed an ice pack and set me up on my couch with a pillow underneath my foot and the ice pack wrapped around my toes. She sat down in the chair next to me and we watched the television for a while. She didn't mention the flag.

"How is it?" she said finally. "How's the pain?"

"There's no pain," I said. "It's just numb."

"Oh, look," she said, pointing at the television.

There was Paul, right in front of my eyes like he'd been all those days in the house, except now he was on the screen. Donna turned up the volume. Paul was sitting with two young boys, trying to explain to them the importance of brushing their teeth. Then a big green space alien tore open the roof and came down with a glowing fluorescent tube and a giant toothbrush. He smiled and his teeth blinded Paul and the children with their brightness. Then the kids looked in the mirror and saw that their teeth were as clean and white as the alien's. They cheered and Paul crossed his arms over his chest and shook his head.

"Well, how about that," Donna said. "I can't believe I know someone famous."

"He's not famous," I said. "It's a commercial."

"But, still. Didn't he want to be famous? Isn't that why he left?"

"He left because he didn't want me anymore."

"That's not true."

I sat up on the couch.

"How do you go on like this, Donna? Tell me the secret." My voice was sharp, and Donna pinched her knees together and her shoulders tensed up. "Really, Donna. I'd like to get inside that head of yours and figure you out."

"I don't appreciate the way you're talking to me," she said. "I'm leaving. I hope your foot feels better."

"God damn it," I said.

She stood up and slapped down her skirt, sending out a puff of loose hair and dust.

"I pray to God you don't think it was worth it," I said. "Do you, Donna?"

She turned to me. Her eyes were sharp as cut glass. I thought I saw it in her—she'd been fighting anger for so long. She put her hands out, and her fingertips shook like little Christmas bells. Then her eyes softened, and I could see she was trying to forgive me for what I'd said. I can't say if she did, only that it seemed to me she was trying.

We haven't spoken since then, but I feel closer to Donna Baker than I ever did before. I know she's there, across the street, with her pain and fantasy, and on certain days when I can't find any peace in what I'm doing, I'll pretend to be Donna and imagine what it must be like to live the way she does.

TO FEEL AGAIN THE KIND
OF LOVE THAT HURTS
SOMETHING TERRIBLE

~~~~~~

KENNY PACED ALONG the driveway, kicking stones, saying to himself, "Finish your milk, finish your homework, finish your prayers."

Huffing, exhausted, he slowly chanted, "Dolphins, dragons, pelicans, trampolines, submarines, jelly beans."

He sat on the lawn with his hands wrapped around his knees and whispered, "Coca-Cola, rock 'n' rolla, supernova . . . shit, shit, shit."

He started over, from the beginning. Because it had to be right, or else everything would go wrong.

Casanova!

He stood up and walked over to the dying maple near the edge of the lawn. Leaves fell in the slight breeze. He plucked a few from the ground, crumpled them in his hand, and shoved the bits into his mouth. The orange ones tasted best. There weren't many orange ones left. It was almost winter.

He turned and shouted toward the house, "Let's get this shucking fo on the road!"

FROM THE bay window, Phil and Mary watched Kenny crush and eat leaves. They used to worry Kenny would get poisoned, but there's only so much you can control.

"Fourteen-year-olds don't eat leaves," Mary said.

"Maybe he's a vegan."

"Tasteless, Phil. Just tasteless."

Going vegan might not be a bad idea for the boy, Phil thought. He was short and chubby, and Mary cut his hair in a way that made his face look like a pale balloon. Some days he was way up. Other days he was way down. One night, a few months back, Mary found a hole in the bathroom wall behind one of her dopey signs about love and light. Phil was in the garage, drinking beer, flipping through an old nudie magazine he'd found behind the seat of his Bobcat. He had had to park the Bobcat after his third DUI. Mary came in from the house and snuck up on Phil sitting in the cage looking at the crumpled spread of a naked woman straddling a fire hydrant.

"When you're done whacking off, I need you to take a look at something," she said, and shut the door.

The hole was the size of a small fist. He reached inside and pulled out a bunch of panties with the tags still on. Some were stuck together.

"He's stealing girls' underwear, and, you know," Mary said.

"I see that."

"Must be in the genes."

Then Kenny punched another boy in the neck. The boy had a condition. He started shaking and foaming at the mouth. Luckily he didn't die.

When Phil asked Kenny why he did it, he said he was trying to save the world from an alien takeover.

"You should be friggin' thanking me," he said.

This was before the meds.

Phil and Mary had taken Kenny out of school and put him in the hospital. Nothing short of a small fortune to watch him solve puzzles and make his bed. But he didn't put any more holes in the walls.

Mary crushed Kenny's pills and sprinkled the dust into his eggs.

"I don't know if this is such a good idea," she said, breathing on Phil's neck as they watched Kenny stomp around in circles outside.

Phil was taking Kenny on his first date. They were going skating at the hockey rink near the bridge.

"Please be good to him," Mary said.

"Why wouldn't I?" he said, pressing a finger against his gums.

"He's very nervous. I can tell."

"He's always nervous. Why'd you let him wear a suit?"

"Look how handsome he is."

"He'll stick out like a—"

Phil's tooth ached so bad he smacked the counter. Mary jumped back, then popped him on the arm.

"You scared me," she said.

"You think *that* was scary?"

In a way he felt nervous for Kenny, felt like he was responsible for making today a day he would remember for the rest of his life. But then, those first few dates with Morgan Price, did he even want to remember them? When they'd gone paddling on boogie boards in the lake behind her house and he kept his shirt on because he was chubby and embarrassed. She had said she liked him because he was different.

"Take your shirt off," she said.

Then the last boy she liked came cruising by on a motorboat and tipped them over on their boards with the swell and blew an air horn and everyone on the lake looked over at Phil standing in the shallow water, his bathing suit bunched up between his legs, waddling like a penguin back up the beach to Morgan's house, his chin quivering. Later, in the kitchen, they quietly nibbled on tuna fish sandwiches with her mother.

SINCE PHIL'S last DUI, they only had the one car. In order to start it now, he had to blow into the Breathalyzer hooked to the dash and wait for the machine to record his blood alcohol level.

He told Kenny that he and Mom were being paid to have someone monitor what type of radio programming they listened to while driving.

"I'm not stupid," Kenny said.

"No, you're not."

"You have a problem."

"Lots of people have problems."

"I know that, too. I saw a woman on TV with no arms and legs. She was like a ball in a chair and she moved the chair around with her mouth."

"That's one kind of problem, sure."

"My problem is mental."

"What do you mean? Where did you hear that?"

"Mom said it. I heard her on the phone. She was telling someone that I had a mental problem."

"She said that?"

"I think it's better than being a ball in a chair, don't you?"

Phil reached over and gently squeezed the back of Kenny's neck.

"You look good in that suit, pal," he said.

"Thanks, I know."

"Girls like a man who dresses nice. When I met your mother, she thought I was a hippie because of how I dressed. I just thought I was rebellious. Anyway, she changed me good."

"I have no idea what you're talking about, Dad."

"Oh, okay, you want to focus, is that it? I'll let you focus."

Phil turned on the radio. He had to keep the sound low because the machine beeped every fifteen minutes, calling him to blow in the tube. Supposedly the engine shut down if he didn't. He wondered what would happen if he were on the highway and forgot, if the car would just stop and he'd get barreled into by a fleet of cars. He hoped he'd survive, because then he'd sue the state and be rich.

Bored with classic rock, Phil had begun listening to jazz. It all sounded like one long song with different pieces. He imagined that the instruments had beating hearts.

"Why are you taking the long way?" Kenny asked.

"What long way? There's only one way, pal. Point A to point B."

"Don't screw with me, Dad."

"Watch it, Kenny."

But what could he say? The kid was smart. And erratic. And possibly dangerous.

They'd been to the rink once before, when the Olympic speed skaters came to Wequaquet for a public exhibition. After that, he taught Kenny how to skate on the pond near their house. Then Kenny always wanted to skate, even when the ice was too thin. Then Phil had to lie about why they couldn't go out, and it broke him a little each time, because he knew Kenny was smart enough to know.

"You want to be a little late," Phil said. "Keep them waiting."

"What if she leaves?"

"She won't. She'll hang around just to let you hear about it."

"Then what?"

"Then you apologize, and take her hand, and apologize again."

"I've never heard you apologize to Mom."

"That's because I don't have to anymore."

Kenny pulled at his crotch and looked out the window. Phil knew he wasn't just worried about being late. He was worried about the world catching fire. He'd been reading about climate change on the Internet. Mary had to take his laptop and tablet and phone away. One night Kenny ran through the house calling, "Code Nine, Code Nine!" He packed the pantry into a duffel bag and the three of them camped in the basement. Mary and Phil played cards while Kenny hugged his knees and rocked back and forth.

The trick, the doctors said, was to acknowledge Kenny's actions but not to engage.

Phil was trying his best to disengage.

IF FRESCA'S going to be there before me, Kenny thought, then I have to find a way to jerk off. He'd been jerking off since last year, when he saw another boy doing it behind a tree at school. The boy had said it was the only way to get rid of all the stuff inside him. Kenny didn't know what stuff the boy was talking about. Not until he practiced. And when he got rid of his stuff, he felt less anxious and his thoughts slowed down and food tasted better. He jerked off in the bathroom stalls and behind the Dunkin' Donuts after school and once right in class through his shorts.

"I have to poo," Kenny told his father.

"Jesus. I thought you didn't want to be late."

"I don't. But I don't want to poo my pants, either. What's the difference? Make her wait longer, right?"

"Not too long. Then she'll probably leave."

"But you said—"

"What the hell do I know, Kenny?"

His father turned in to an Exxon station.

"Be quick," he said.

In the bathroom stall, Kenny thought about Fresca's dark hair and wide eyebrows and her skin, a butter-cream color like a toffee candy. She called Kenny "Kenbo." He liked that name. It made him sound like he was some kind of karate master. He would sit behind her in class. She wore low-cut jeans, and he could see her thongs. She liked bright colors. It didn't take him long to come after picturing her skating around in her fluorescent-green underwear.

PHIL WATCHED as a car pulled up behind him and out came Coach Linnehan, all bug-eyed and mournful, standing at the pump and studying the screen as though it were an Egyptian hieroglyph.

At least he wasn't that bad off. Not yet, anyway.

When he and Mary had started out, it felt like he'd been drugged with joy. Overwhelmed by the insane happiness of New. Colors seemed brighter, simple objects made him curious, days flew by and exploded into dust like clay pigeons.

He watched Coach Linnehan slide his card in and out of the slot at the pump. Such simple desperation made him feel better.

Kenny hopped back in the car, smelling like gas fumes and cheap soap.

Phil blew into the Breathalyzer tube and started the engine.

"So what's this girl's name?" he asked.

"Francesca," Kenny said.

"That pretty little Jew girl?"

"So what if she's Jewish?"

"Right. Of course."

"She likes to be called Fresca. That's her favorite soda. I hope the machine at the rink has it."

Phil remembered how when Kenny was a baby he'd fall or bang his head on something and get this terrified look in his eyes, and his mouth would open and his face would scrunch up, but he wouldn't cry, he wouldn't make a sound, then, all of a sudden, like an archer stretching a bow to its limit and finally releasing the arrow, he would scream, and the sound would cut through the house with so much velocity it felt as if he'd pierced Phil's breastplate.

IT WAS hard to get anything on girls like Fresca; sometimes what you got was by not trying to get anything at all. She was always surrounded by her two equally beautiful friends, Alex and Sara. But Fresca had green eyes instead of blue and brown, and her hair was long and wavy instead of short and straight, and maybe it wasn't that she was so beautiful after all, maybe it was how when she looked at you it was like she trapped your entire life force in her gaze.

So it was pure luck when a few weeks ago Kenny had been sitting outside against the cafeteria wall trying to make his thumb disappear when he heard this voice like a cat being stretched apart. He went over to the recess in the wall near the dumpsters, and there was Fresca with pink pods in her ears, eyes closed, singing some shitty pop song. Watching her without her knowing, it was like she became real to him, not like the girl who rolled her eyes in math class or flirted with Dean Vechionni, the fat lesbo warlord who nixed wearing baseball hats and hooded sweatshirts at school because they were places kids might hide weapons.

Fresca freaked when she saw Kenny, pulled the pods from her ears, and cornered him against the wall.

"Don't you tell anyone about this," she said.

"It wasn't that bad," he lied.

"Why are you smiling? Don't smile. You're going to tell. I know it. You freak. God."

Her breath smelled like nectarines. He grabbed her hair and kissed her and she pushed him off, hard against the wall, and he fell on his butt and bruised his tailbone. He had to use Mom's heating pad for the next three nights while he thought of a way to get close enough to Fresca to kiss her again.

The next day, when he passed her in the hall, she was the only one of her friends who actually looked at him. He could tell she was nervous, not about how he was walking bent over because of the bruised tailbone, but about her singing and if he had told anyone. Who would I tell? he thought. And why would they believe me? Then he realized it would be pretty easy to trick her into thinking he was going to tell.

After math class he snuck up behind her and said, "You know I recorded your performance on my phone."

She stopped and her friends stopped. They looked at Kenny like he was a puke stain on the wall.

"You're not allowed to have a phone on school grounds," she said.

Another one of Dean Vech's laws.

"What's he talking about, Fres?" her friend Alex said.

So Fresca had a nickname for her nickname. He said it over and over before going to sleep that night.

"Nothing. He's mental," Fresca said.

"You stink like a dead fish," Alex said.

"Ever heard of deodorant?" the other girl, Sara, said.

"Yes, I've heard of—"

But they were already halfway down the hall, arms locked with a couple of no-neck Red Raiders wearing their Friday game shirts.

After school, near the number-five bus, he felt a hard flick against his earlobe.

"Okay, what do you want?" Fresca asked.

"I want to see you outside of school," Kenny said, rubbing his ear.

"Like where? Where can I see you and not be seen by anyone else? And don't say your room. I can't imagine what kind of weirdo stuff you have in there."

"I don't have weirdo stuff. I have normal stuff."

Except for the panties he stole from MegaWorld, which he kept adding to every weekend. That was probably pretty weird.

"How about the skating rink?"

She looked over her shoulder, then stood on her tiptoes and looked over his head.

"Fine. But you have to swear you'll erase that video."

"I swear," he said.

"You have to swear on something."

Kenny raised his right hand.

"I swear on my right hand; may it always stay attached to my arm."

"God, you're such a freak-o," she said, and walked off.

PHIL'S FATHER had been a pilot. His heart stopped while he was flying from Chicago to Anchorage. He had never flown that route before but had agreed to take it on to keep his job.

Phil thought that, seeing the icecaps from fifteen thousand feet that first time, his father's body was unable to sustain the beauty. Lucky for the passengers, the copilot was able to land the plane. Phil imagined that time stopped like that, when you see something so beautiful, something like love. He felt that the first time he saw Mary. Maybe all the years between then and now had been his attempt to get back to that one moment of clarity.

But he didn't know where to begin.

He looked at Kenny.

"Stop biting your nails," he said.

"I wasn't."

"Your thumbnail's hanging by a thread."

Kenny tore it off and sucked on it like he did when he was a baby. Phil hadn't been able to help but feel anything other than joy. His little guy all bundled up with his thumb in his mouth, making those cooing sounds, dreaming of what? What does a baby dream of?

"Let me see," he said.

Kenny showed him his thumb, the blood speckled behind the nail.

"That'll dry up before we get there."

"I hope so."

"You need to start working in the yard. Your hands are too soft. Girls don't like a guy with soft hands. I had to tar foundations when I was a kid. Heat up the tar with kindling and an iron grate, then bring the buckets down the stepladder into the hole, over a hundred degrees down there if not more, sweating, painting on the hot tar, hands blistering up. That was work. And when I was with your mother, she knew I—"

"Dad! Please!"

"What?"

"I so don't want to hear about you and Mom and whatever you two did."

"I'm talking about love, Kenny. Women. How they need to be held and touched and talked to. You need to know these things if you want to have a chance with this girl."

He stopped at a traffic light and looked at Kenny looking out the window at the floating dancers in front of Big Tim's Auto Emporium.

"Kenny?"

"Yeah, Dad."

"Did you hear what I said?"

KENNY PANICKED when the Breathalyzer machine began beeping just as Fresca and her mother pulled into the next space over. His father was literally breathing into a long plastic dick-tube with his cheeks puffed out. Maybe Fresca didn't notice, because in no time she and her mom were at the door to the rink. Fresca held the laces of her skates with the precision of a puppeteer; they already seemed to be spinning on the ice.

"That her?" his father asked, placing the Breathalyzer back in its holster.

"Yep."

"She's pretty. And her mom's not half bad, either."

"Please."

"Oh, shit, Kenny. Just two guys talking. How much does it cost to skate around in circles these days?"

"I don't know."

Kenny took the mangled bills plus some change and pocket debris.

"That should do."

When Kenny went to open the door, his father put his hand on his arm, just holding it there, his fingers pressing lightly into his biceps. He wasn't looking at Kenny. He was looking in the rearview mirror. Kenny turned and saw some garbage heaped up against the cement slabs in front of the parking spaces.

"Dad?" he said.

His father let go of his arm.

"All right, kiddo," he said. "Go get 'em."

MARY WAS so deep in the past, Phil thought, but also right here, so close he felt like he could grab hold of her waist, and then what?

Hang on for dear life.

Never complain.

Never say a negative thing about her hair or clothing or weight.

Kiss her in the morning and at night and when she least expected to be kissed, when she was just in from the yard or finished washing dishes.

Take Sundays off to drive out somewhere beautiful and remark on how beautiful it was.

Finally go on that picnic. Make the sandwiches, pack the basket, find a soft pad of grass in the shade.

Shower together.

Make love slow and heavy and fall asleep naked with the smell of sex hovering over their spent bodies.

Do it all over again, better and better, like practice for a game that will never be played.

Because now, every day he was going home to her but not her, a version of her he had built out of fears and mistakes. He wanted her to know how much he missed being in love. Could he tell her that? Just that one thing?

Today, he thought. Today my life could change forever.

But the car wouldn't start. He blew into the plastic tube again and the machine beeped and he tried the ignition, but nothing sparked. He picked up the Breathalyzer and broke it against the dashboard. The robotic female voice sighed and died.

His tooth hurt so bad he tried to punch it out of his mouth. The punch numbed the pain.

"When you fall," his father used to say, "get back up again, unless some big black bastard is standing over you. Then you stay down."

His father had a way with words.

Phil wanted to die like he did, staring straight into the beautiful.

ONCE HE saw Fresca on the bench, lacing up her skates, Kenny got a boner. And because he'd grown out of his suit since Grandpa's funeral, you could see the boner sticking straight out like an arrowhead.

Before he had time to cover it, Fresca looked over and said, "Ew, gross."

But she smiled when she said it, and laughed.

He sat down and put on his hockey skates.

"Nice suit," she said.

"Thanks. I know it's weird."

"It's not weird. It just doesn't go with your skates."

"Oh."

"Hey, what about me?"

"What about you?"

"Jesus, you're a nut job."

"How you look, you mean?"

"Duh."

"You always look good. I can't stand it, you look so good."

She glanced at him. Her face candy-pink.

Then she was through the gate and on the ice. Kenny raced past her, forward and backward, and as she spun in a slow circle, he circled her. She reached out and grabbed hold of his arms and they spun together, and she let go and they skated around awhile and met up near the boards on the far side behind the nets. That's where she kissed him, kissed him with her nectarine breath filling his nose, kissed him so soft he slipped and fell on his butt again, but this time it didn't hurt so bad.

PHIL COULDN'T remember the last time he cried. Last time must've been when Mary told him she was pregnant. No, it was when he had found out they were having a boy. He was happiest then. He got that same feeling seeing Kenny and that pretty Jewish girl kissing on the ice.

An hour and three beers later, Francesca's mother returned.

Phil didn't feel like explaining about the situation.

"We'd really appreciate a ride," he said, and looked at Kenny. But Kenny didn't seem embarrassed.

He was flying. He was in love.

Nothing hurt so bad.

On the way home, riding in the back of Francesca's mother's Jeep Liberty, Phil put his hand on Kenny's knee and mussed up his hair.

"My baby boy," he said, softly and without regret.

DOWNHILL

~~~~

EVERY SO OFTEN my little boy, Jasper, will ask me what the sky looks like. I used to be creative, but after a while you realize that what you're creating is only relative to what you've already created. One cloud looks like a bulldog. Then, what does a bulldog look like? Then, what does Grandpa look like? Lately I've been struggling with similes. We've had nothing but gray sunless days here. The ground is trapped under mounds of snow, and the relentless cold charges every person in town with a certain kind of dread and fear.

Jasper was born blind. He's four years old now and very curious. I make up a lot of things. Like when we listen to music in the car and I tell him there're little men inside the stereo playing tiny instruments just for us.

"What do they eat?" he asks.

"Smaller portions of what we eat."

"How do you feed them?"

"With a tiny fork."

"Do they ever come out?"

"Sure, when they need a break."

"Can I hold one?"

"Be careful."

I shut off the radio and take his hand. It's the tip of my finger forming infinity signs in his palm.

"What happens when he gets older and starts finding out what's true and what's not?" Darlene asked me one night after a gang of thugs threw a rock through our living room window for no apparent reason other than to make us feel what they felt. I told Jasper that the rush of air coming through his play circle was a flock of birds flying above us. He ran around the living room, jumping up and trying to grab at them. It was beautiful.

"Better he imagines the world this way while he can, don't you think?" I said to Darlene.

She knows it is possible Jasper might never see at all. Our medical bills are through the roof. We've maxed out our credit cards and the house is in foreclosure. Life for Darlene and me is a long, frozen march between home and work, the grocery store and the hospital. But not for Jasper. As far as he knows, we go everywhere. In the summer, it's the beaches in Spain (a polluted lake near the highway). In winter, it's the mountains in Switzerland (a hill near my old high school). Go to sleep, I say. When you wake up, the plane will already be on the ground.

The next step is corneal-transplant surgery in both eyes. I don't even want to tell you how much that's going to cost. It's like, I'm reading online about how these kids from New Guinea and Paraguay get this free surgery and they're watching TV and playing with crayons, and I'm thinking, What about Jasper? How broke do I have to be?

On this day, one week before Christmas, I'm lucky to have

just sold a used 2005 Honda Accord to a young couple that seems to have that same spark Darlene and I had when we first got married. So, all things considered, I'm having a pretty decent morning when Big Tim comes into the showroom and says, "Did you hear about those five North Koreans shot to death trying to cross over into China?"

This is the last thing I need to be thinking about right now.

"I didn't hear," I say.

"No? It was all over the news. Seems like every good citizen of the planet should keep up with what's going on in the world, Falachi. It *might* make you a better salesman."

"I just closed a deal before you walked in."

"For that beater?" He looks out the showroom window at the newlyweds, who are staring at the hood of the Honda uncertainly. "Hardly a game changer."

"I need to get my commission check by this afternoon, if that's okay?"

"Hmm," Big Tim says, stroking his chin. He used to have a beard, but then he read somewhere that Americans don't trust men with beards anymore. "I'll see what I can do."

Last Christmas, I wasn't able to get Darlene anything. I made a card and used a coupon for free perennials from Stop & Shop. For Jasper I stole a toy truck from the playroom next to the repair shop. It was all scratched up and a wheel was broken off and the little horn got stuck when he pushed on the steering wheel so this long, intolerable wail sounded and made him cry. I tried to fix it but ended up smacking the thing against the coffee table until it broke. I did my best to paste some of the parts together and make the sounds that a truck would make: a high-pitched *beep* when he backed it up, a *vroom vroom* when he pushed it forward, a rumbling motor when he let it go.

"See," Big Tim says, "the thing about the Koreans is that it turns out one of them wasn't completely dead. They shot him in the stomach so he'd have to suffer. When the human-aid workers found him, he wasn't able to speak and they didn't have the capabilities to save him, so *they* had to kill him. How do you think that makes those people feel, Falachi?"

"It sounds awful," I say, not paying full attention.

"It *is* awful!" he says. "What about the missing girl they found in a dumpster in Albuquerque? She'd been gone a week. The search was called off. Then it turns out these two maniacs who lived in her neighborhood had kidnapped her. She wasn't more than three blocks away. The things they did to her! You know what the girl's father said? 'She's in heaven now.' Exact quote."

Does it make me a bad person if I don't care all that much about the North Koreans or the dead girl in Albuquerque? Or every other bad thing you see and read and hear about? Maybe. But what can I say besides, wow, God, Jesus, damn?

"Don't even get me started on Mexico," he says. "Heads are rolling in the streets of Juárez. Like, *actually rolling down streets*."

"Jesus."

"Have you ever seen a rolling head, Falachi?"

When Big Tim gets worked up like this, crying is inevitable. He lets out a long whine and starts choking up to catch his breath. A string of spit hangs off his bottom lip and this little bubble forms between his lips. Once it pops, that whine starts again.

"It's all right, Tim. You're not responsible."

"Oh, no? You don't think? We're human, Falachi. Human! Those killers and rapists, they're human, too."

"But it's Christmas, and we've got this big promotion going, and I think things are going to get better."

"Have you seen our sales? Do you have any idea how much

money I owe the bank? The government? It can't get any worse, is that what you're saying? Because if that's what you're saying, oh, boy, you better prepare yourself."

Big Tim covers his eyes with the sleeve of his suit jacket and heads to the bathroom so none of the other salesmen can see him. His sobs echo through the showroom. It's a good thing we don't have any customers.

A bum wanders in and pours a cup of coffee, sits in the lounge, and thumbs through a golf magazine. Some high school kids draw penises in the frost on the plate-glass windows. Plows pass by in a row, like military vehicles. The used Honda is the first car I've sold in a month. We've had snow for three weeks straight. My mornings have been spent scraping ice off windshields, running the engines, laying down salt. Jeff and Luis haven't sold a car since summer. Their eyelids are yellow and puffy from lack of sleep. Jeff took a second job as a telemarketer. On Sundays, he plays Santa Claus at the mall. Luis's wife divorced him and he had to move out of the colonial they bought a few years ago to his cousin's place in the Heights, which if you've ever been to the Heights you'd know is a big step down from anyplace else. I'm twenty thousand dollars in debt and Darlene has been threatening to leave and take Jasper to live with her parents in Florida. She has faith in me, but faith only goes so far, especially when the old days keep getting older and your memory of them isn't quite the same anymore.

So the commission check is a pretty big deal.

A few minutes later, Big Tim's looking much better. He's wet and combed his hair, and his face is no longer flushed. He scans the vacant showroom before walking into his office. Swirls of snow sweep across the front lot. Jeff is playing hearts on his computer. Luis is staring at the fish. The aquarium tank was meant as a way to keep kids entertained while we went over the numbers with their parents in one of our cubicles. It's a monster, close to eighty gallons, with dozens of tropical fish: striped tiger barbs, neon tetras, zebra danios, white clouds. Problem is, none of them seem to be moving.

"Are they dead?" I ask Luis.

"They were dead, but if you stare at them long enough, they start moving again. It's like a miracle."

"We need to call someone."

"Yes, a priest."

"Falachi!" Big Tim shouts from his office. "Come here. I want you to see something."

"Really," I say to Luis. "Get on the horn and have this tank taken out of here."

It's hard to get comfortable in Big Tim's office. His old high school trophies and a collection of photographs from his playing days are on display in a glass case against the wall, and over in the corner is a full-size cardboard cutout of him with his arms flexed and two Playmates squeezing his biceps. He used to be the local Bud Man back in the eighties. On his desk are more-recent photographs of him with his ex-wife and their adopted son, Brutus. Looking around the room is like looking at the devolution of Big Tim when you finally let your eyes settle on him in the flesh.

"Watch this," he says.

On his computer screen is a still shot of a large crowd in some market in Asia. Big Tim pushes PLAY and the crowd begins to move. The camerawork is shaky. You can hear sirens and car horns and bells and this eerie crackling sound that must be a hundred or so people and animals and scooters making noise at the same time. Then a man crosses in front of the camera and bursts into flames. There's this massive *pop* like an engine backfiring. The man runs into the market, and people are screaming and trying to get out of his way. He falls to the ground, flailing. Someone tosses a blanket over his body, but the fire eats through the blanket. Finally, a man blasts him with a fire extinguisher. I can't tell if he's dead or alive. The video ends.

Tim plays it back.

"Listen," he says. "Is the cameraman laughing?"

"Maybe he's nervous," I say. "Tim . . . if I can get that check—"

"Look, he doesn't even attempt to save the guy. And see this here on the side? There're all these links to videos of exploding people. If this many people are exploding while someone happens to have a camera going, think about how many are exploding when there's *no* camera."

"Come on, Tim. Let's take a deep breath."

But it's too late. He chucks a stress ball in the shape of a clown's head across the room and begins to whine. I can already see Darlene packing up what little we have left. I shut the blinds around his office and close the door behind me. Everyone can hear him, though. This has been going on for a while now. Part of the reason there's such low energy in the showroom.

"Don't let anyone see him like this," I tell Suzy, his secretary, an old, callous woman whose refusal to pity Tim might be the only thing keeping the place afloat.

She looks up from her computer screen.

"He's already sent these videos of exploding people to everyone in the building," she says.

"Damn."

"You know what I think? Men are bigger babies than actual babies. When a baby falls, it gets up and looks at you with this kind of stunned amazement. Grown men, they just keep falling."

I picture Jasper on the beach in Florida, the water creeping up the shoreline toward his small, ticklish body. Maybe it's the hands of thousands of sea creatures trying to pull him down into their secret world. Maybe the crashing waves are really falling buildings. Maybe when he leaps into my arms, it doesn't have to be him saving me.

"I'm at lunch," I tell Suzy.

I walk through the repair shop, where the mechanics are sitting on tires, playing cards on the flat side of a big wooden spool. There're no cars in the bays. We were given a bad name last spring when Channel 5 sent an investigative reporter into the shop to have his brakes looked at. The mechanics told him he needed to have new brakes put in, and while they were at it, they took a look at the transmission, and that needed to be replaced, too. But there was nothing wrong with the car's brakes, and the transmission was just fine. The piece ran on their weekly report "BUSTED!" Big Tim came off real bad, pushing one of the cameramen into the giant inflatable air dancers we had lined up outside the dealership. "From high school football star to scamming you on your car, Tim Tucker gets *busted!*" the reporter said, just before Tim lowered his shoulder and drove him into the ground.

Outside in the back lot is where we keep the real clunkers. Jeff is getting stoned in the front seat of his used Mercury, which has two broken taillights and a garbage bag ripped and taped over the passenger-side window. Seeing Jeff in his car like this, I can't help but wonder what the hell is going to happen to all of us. He's been wilting like a sun-starved cactus ever since Jamaica Man, the local tanning salon, went under. His skin is a pale, sticky-looking hue now, and he's lost a good twenty pounds, which I think has more to do with his lack of sales.

Big Tim is convinced Jeff is dying. Last month he invited all the boys out to Tally-Hoes on Industrial and we had to pony up twenty bucks apiece for a dark-skinned girl named Chardonnay to straddle Jeff and call him Papa Bear. "When you're dying, nothing's better than a pair of tits in your face," Big Tim said. It did seem to make everything bearable for a few days after.

"How you feeling, Jeff?"

"Better than ever," he says, and passes the pipe out the window toward me.

"No, thanks."

"It's your reality."

"What about putting a good word in for me with the telemarketers?"

"People are actually standing in line to sit there and take a beating all night for less than eight bucks an hour, and you want to be a part of it?"

"I'm in a bind this season."

"There're better ways to make a buck."

"You mean illegal ways."

"Who's really watching us, partner?"

"What's your plan?"

"You're looking at it."

"You want to rob Big Tim?"

"The insurance will cover whatever we take. It's foolproof."

"Then what?"

"Then we live in paradise."

A world Jasper can see. The long strip of white sand stretching the length of the Caribbean, the blue water and tropical fish; maybe the red rocks out west, the smooth canyon walls, the twinkling stars at twilight. I feel colder than ever and fold my arms tightly across my chest.

"Falach? Are you listening? You could be the lookout. Just like a real heist. We could get a truck in here on Christmas Eve, no problemo."

Listening to Jeff, I can understand why Darlene thinks fantasies are dangerous.

"I'm not a criminal," I say.

"Jesus, man, you really have no idea what's going on. Always keeping your head up, but never looking side to side. Just think about it."

I walk toward the high school where I went twenty years ago. Back then I thought I'd make it further than working at the car dealership next door. When Darlene and I got together, we looked at a map of the country and picked out where we wanted to live once we had enough money: somewhere out west, in the mountains, with a city close by. Then things started piling up. When I was making good money, it didn't make sense to leave, and when I started making no money, we couldn't leave. Trapped in this inertia, you look forward to the holidays.

I remember those Christmases when my father would take me to the noontime movie, some shoot-'em-up that was much easier to forget than his tall, lean body standing outside the theater, smoking cigarettes, calling his bookie to get the spreads on the games that afternoon. I don't think he ever watched a movie straight through. When it was finished, I'd find him resting in the car. "Ready to go, chief?" he'd say. "How was it?" As he drove back through the whirls of snow and chimney smoke, I described every detail I could remember, learning to condense information into neat packages, to invent what I'd forgotten. To change just one thing meant I had to change everything. Mom was home cleaning up the pine needles under the tree, folding the clothes given to me by aunts and uncles, checking on the turkey, playing

Christmas carols on the stereo. My father stretched out on the sofa, setting the new watch she had given him.

A young boy in snow pants and an oversize wool cap is halfway up the steep hill near the practice field behind the school, pushing his boots into the hardening snow, dragging a plastic sled. At the crest of the hill is a row of snowy pines where I found a dead cat last fall with the name *Julio* shaved crudely into her fur.

When the boy reaches the top, he sets the sled on the plateau and, before getting in, waves to me, and I wave back. Standing there with my hands in my pockets, watching the boy fly down the hill, I can feel my eyes well up from the rush of air, the free fall. I remember the tiered hillside behind my uncle's house, where we went for Christmas Eve dinner. There was a lake at the end of the hill. My older cousins were all hockey players and set up goals and skated effortlessly while my younger cousin, Randy, and I took turns on the sled, seeing how much speed we could generate by bending our bodies into bullets, how close to the lake we could get. Once, I put my head between my knees and Randy pushed me with all his strength and the metal skis of the sled zipped through the fresh, powdery snow, and at that speed, I thought, there was no way I'd get held up at the bottom. The snow climbed up over me like a wave, and in that last moment, I looked up and realized the sled had veered off course and was headed toward the playground set in the backyard. I tried to pull up on the brake handles at my sides, but it was too late. The braking sent me headlong into the metal pole on the side of the swings. I knocked out one of my teeth and split my bottom lip, which stiffened into an awkward pout as I trudged back up to the house. The adults were concerned at first, but later, at dinner, when they were half-drunk and in good spirits, they laughed at how swollen my lip had gotten. They called me Monkey Lip.

The boy makes a tiny shriek when the sled hits a mogul. The sled bounces and he's able to straighten it and finish the run by spinning ninety degrees, stopping just before he reaches the sidewalk. What unappreciated talents we develop at that age! He's red-faced and wide-eyed, and his hat has gone crooked on his head. I have the impulse to reach out and fix it for him.

"Hey, buddy!" someone shouts from behind me. I turn to see a tall, broad-shouldered guy in a heavy winter coat walking toward me.

"What are you, like, checking out my kid?"

"What's that? No. What do you mean?"

"You're standing here with this goofy grin on your face."

"No, that's not it. That's not it at all."

"What, then? You just come out to watch boys sled down hills?"

He's got a face like an anvil, cigarette smoke on his breath, a blackened front tooth. A real man, it seems, from not so long ago.

"Look, I'm sorry you got that impression. I was just remembering what it was like to be his age, you know? I got excited, that's all."

"I'll fucking bet, pal." He's balled up his fist and my hands are raised slightly, prepared for the blow. "If the boy weren't here, I'd kick your ass," he says.

The logic doesn't make sense, but I'm relieved when he unclenches his fist and grabs his son by the wrist, pulling him off the sled. The boy cries. His father picks him up and puts him over his shoulder.

"It's okay, sweetie," he says.

Snot is coming out of the boy's nose, freezing around the

edges of his nostrils. His father pats him on the back and walks off toward the parking lot.

They forget the sled.

Maybe a kind gesture would keep them from thinking of me as a pedophile for the rest of their lives. But it's almost perfect, with just a few dings and scrapes along the plastic siding.

When I was a boy, my friends and I carried metal trash-can lids to the tops of hills and gave each other a great shove forward. We fell and tumbled and broke bones. We were in it for the gratification we got on crisp winter afternoons, for the hot chocolate in the backseat of mom's car, for the homemade sauce cooking on the stove at home. That was Christmas in America. *That* was paradise.

No matter where it comes from, Jasper deserves the same joy I had.

Sitting on my lap at the top of the hill, he'll feel the wind in his face and my arms tighten around his body. Don't worry, little guy. Nothing bad is going to happen. You're going to feel this rush just before the end, as if we're flying through the sky. It'll be scary the first time, but you'll want to do it all over again once we're at the bottom.

Remember that, I'll tell him, as we drag the sled up the hill. And everything else I've told you, too.

FRIEND OF MINE

~~~~~~

I WAS ON the porch watching these two cute-as-hell bunnies
in Coach Linnehan's yard playing this game where they stared
each other down until one of them sprinted forward and the
other hopped up to avoid the inevitable collision. Then they
turned and stared off again and kept at it until the one sprint-
ing caught the other so that it was his turn to be the hopper. I
was thinking about how I used to play games like that and
couldn't remember when I stopped playing those games and
how as kids we must've invented them from watching little animals, and that's all I was when I was young, a little animal, but
then I started having all this shit thrown at me about what I
was supposed to be and what I needed to do to be it and how I
could keep on being it if I did certain things, certain right things,
and at one point my head must have basically exploded so I
couldn't do anything and I couldn't get back to that time when
I was a kid playing those little animal games.

It's rare I get a moment where I can remember what it was like to be who I was then, hopping around, playing games, not thinking about anything. Watching those rabbits, I felt at peace for the first time in a long time. In my heart, I'm saying. I felt calm.

Then Coach Linnehan comes out onto his front steps and shoots both rabbits in the gut with his nine millimeter.

"What the hell, Coach," I shout from the porch. "They were just playing around."

"Damn buggers eat up my gazanias," he says.

"Look at the one on the right. He's all twitching and shit."

Coach sights it with the gun and splatters his head with a bullet.

"Only decent thing I could do," he says.

"You could've not shot them in the first place."

"They ate my gazanias."

"Fuck your gazanias," I say, looking at the bunnies, their insides now soaking his perfectly trimmed lawn. "You totally ruined my morning."

I USED to play ball for Coach Linnehan when I was in high school. I was a guard on the offensive line and I had a quick first step, which was necessary when we ran trap plays and I had to take out the defensive end on the other side of the line. Then I crunched my neck my senior year and missed the last five games of the season. Coach recommended me to some small schools in the area based on my performance during junior year, but my grades were bad and I had to take summer school just to graduate and I honestly didn't have the heart to play anymore. Sometimes I still feel this little twinge in my neck.

After I got out of high school I was hanging around town, living with my parents, working as a landscaper with my buddy Justin, who ended up renting a little place in the Heights, right next to Coach. He let me move in to split rent. Justin had barely graduated, too, and was training for the Army, getting strong and lean, drinking these protein shakes that made his sweat smell like manure. After work we'd sit out on the porch and drink beer and, before Justin enlisted, smoke a little pot and listen to Pearl Jam, and once it got past a certain time Coach would come out standing there in his tight shorts and stained T-shirt with his little bitch tits hanging to the sides, looking like some old-timey asshole, chewing on the end of a cigar, saying we had no taste in music, or culture, and how would we define the word *legacy*, did we even know what a legacy was?

"You two are never going to make it," he'd say.

By that time his authority meant nothing. We laughed like hell and turned the music up louder and kept going till daylight, when it was time to gas up the mowers and mix the oil for the Weedwackers, toss the rakes and leaf blowers and pitchforks in the back of the truck, and drive to a job site. Then we'd smash a few energy drinks and drop some Visine in our eyes, slap each other in the face, and work like dogs, digging up roots, transplanting rhododendrons, mowing lawns as short and perfect as a country-club fairway. When we finished, we went to the packy, stocked up, dumped the beer in a cooler, drove down to the lake, and watched the fifteen-year-old girls swim in circles while we got buzzed, then hit a bar or two looking for chicks our own age. We usually ended up back on the porch, in that cool summer night breeze, talking shit about what I can't remember, but sincere enough that once in a while

Justin or I would break down and we'd hug it out and say thanks for listening to all that. Then we'd blast the music and call out plays until Coach slammed his window shut.

But during that summer, I always had it in the back of my mind what Coach said about making it. What did he mean by making it? I felt pretty good about the way my life was going: I had cash in my wallet, and the weather was perfect, and sometimes I got laid, and other times I was so tired I went right to sleep without thinking about anything. I guess I had dreamed of playing professional ball at one point, but what the hell for, when all these guys are drooling from their mouths at age forty, asking their wives where they are, not remembering fuck all from the past.

When I was even younger, I wanted to be a fireman, because the local fire chief came to our class to teach us CPR and told us a story about how he saved this little girl from a burning apartment complex. There was so much smoke and he was so full of fear, but he didn't care, because that was his job and his responsibility and he was prepared to give his life up for this girl, and once he had her in his arms and brought her out of the smoke, he asked her, "Where's your mother?" but she was coughing and couldn't speak and pointed to the apartment, and so he went back into the fire and found the girl's mother pinned against the wall of her bedroom by a piece of fallen ceiling. He pushed the piece of ceiling out of the way, picked the woman up, and put her over his shoulder, even grabbed a half-burned stuffed animal lying in the hallway, and got her out before the floor fell through. It was such a powerful fucking story, and the guy had the stuffed animal, this floppy-eared dog with a stitch in its eye and a toasted paw, which was his endgame, I guess, because all of us were pretty much stunned, little shits that we were, and a few of the girls had tears in their eyes. The fire chief passed around the stuffed dog as evidence that this happened. While we touched its burned, prickly head, he stroked his big gray mustache and said if we were interested in one day becoming firemen or firewomen, this was the kind of reward we'd get. We'd get to save lives.

I don't know when I stopped wanting to be a fireman. It's not like I couldn't go up to the community college and learn to be one if I wanted. It's just that I don't care so much anymore about saving lives, considering there're so many pieces of shit in this world and you might save some life that doesn't deserve to be saved, and this someone goes on to do something completely fucked up, and you have to live with the guilt that you were the one who kept him in the world when it was all set for him to burn.

But I still wanted to know what making it was, how I could make it, why Coach Linnehan believed he had made it and was in a position to be critical of those he felt weren't making it. He coached the Wequaquet Red Raiders to three championship seasons during his fifteen-year tenure and finally retired after his second consecutive losing season, when people around town were saying he didn't have it anymore, had lost his focus when his daughter died and his wife left him not long after. He was usually alone, except for when he went out on Thursday nights and brought home some divorcée that clearly couldn't stand straight, and who knows what kind of lovemaking they did in there, because Justin and I could only hear this horrible, ear-splitting jazz coming from his bedroom. Other nights he would smoke his cigar on his porch and read these giant biographies of ex-presidents like Jefferson and Nixon, and occasionally he'd drop in some quote when criticizing us. He told us Nixon had said, "There's always the day before the day everything changes." Justin nodded and stroked his chin and said, "I'll eat your face off, Linnehan."

In a way I felt sorry for Coach, even if he was a complete douchebag, and I guess that maybe making it meant just making it for a while so that you had some idea what it was.

TOWARD THE end of summer, Justin stopped staying up late with me, quit drinking beer and smoking weed, ran ten miles every morning before we even got in the truck, all so he could fly through basic training and get his ass blown up in Iraq. At least, that's what I told him, because I didn't want him to leave and I didn't like the way he was changing, and it hit me that maybe what Coach had said about the day before the day everything changed had got to him, even when he brushed it off the way he did, because it was around that time we sort of drifted apart.

The week before Justin was deployed, Coach left a copy of *The Art of War* on our front stoop, a book that he had read from as part of his pre-game pep talks. We would smash our fists against our helmets, Coach holding the book high like some kind of preacher, all of us growling and barking, and Coach howling a prophetic affirmation, something like, Invincibility lies in the defense; the possibility of victory in the attack! By the time he opened up the big metal door to the locker room and we saw the lights on the field, we were ready to tear apart the other team and anyone associated with them.

EVER SINCE that summer Justin left, I've been waiting for the day when everything will change, thinking yesterday was the day before this day, which is the day I've been waiting for. But nothing has really changed, except for what's gone on in the world, which I don't have any control over and is just a bunch of fucked-up shit I don't want to think about anyway.

Then today I see the two bunnies playing their bunny game and I'm like, That's it! That's the thing! But Coach comes out and smokes both of them without giving two damns how it might affect him or me or anyone else who might've seen it (some neighbors are outside looking around after hearing the shots) and how it obviously affected the bunnies. He's standing there with the gun in his hand, lowered to his side, his pudgy belly quivering, and with his free hand he catches the step and sits down, places the gun at his side, and puts his head in his hands and starts sobbing like some kid with no friends, which I'm thinking is a good reason to cry, because ever since Justin left I've been feeling real lonely, sometimes talking to him even though he's not here.

"Coach?" I finally say.

He doesn't move. It's not like I'm going to go over there and hold the guy, but I don't go back inside, either. I turn on some music and drink my coffee and watch him until he eventually collects himself and goes around back and returns with a shovel, scoops up the bunnies, and puts them in a black garbage bag.

"I probably didn't have to shoot them," he says, loud enough for me to hear.

"You did what you had to, I guess," I say.

Then he looks at me as if he's never seen me before, and I'm thinking maybe there's something wrong upstairs, something he can't control. Half the neighbors are on the street, staring at him holding the bag with the dead bunnies in it, his eyes red and puffy and the brilliant sunburst of his gazania plot intact. I'm thinking he just needed to let off some steam, which is something I can understand, because sometimes I'll go down to the basement and punch Justin's old heavy bag until my hands are sore and I'm tired and hungry and don't feel so much rage over what I can't control.

But Coach is still standing there like a statue. I turn off the music and walk across the lawn, carefully stepping over his gazanias. First I put the gun in the back of my jeans. Then I take the bag from his hand.

I say, "Let's go inside, Coach."

"All right, Mac," he says, half here, half out there. "Let's go inside."

SOME FUNKY brown streaks on the walls from all his cigar smoking, clothes thrown over the stair handrail, dirty plates on the coffee table: all the signs of a man alone. I'd never been inside, but I recognize the trophies on his mantel from our championship run, polished to a fine metallic glow. There's a row of framed photographs of his daughter as a baby, a girl, and a teenager, the last one in black and white, an action photo of her in mid-stride, legs stretched like wings, forever suspended above the glow of the studio floor. We used to joke about her—you know, kid stuff, how her flexibility was something to admire. Then there're some taken by his ex-wife, I'm guessing, of the two of them together, one of them at Wequaquet Beach behind some shitty, misshapen sand castles, and another of them trying to catch up to the pack during a three-legged race. Who knew the fat bastard ever smiled?

"I need a maid," he says.

I put down the bag of bunnies, then I pull the gun out of my jeans and empty the clip—something Justin taught me when we went shooting at the reservation last summer—put

the clip in my pocket, and place the gun on the end table next
to the couch.

Coach carries the bag of bunnies into the kitchen. I wonder
why I was so frightened of him when I was in high school. Why
just his voice made my nerves coil, or even his slow walk out
to the center of the field at the end of practice, twirling and un-
twirling his whistle around his forefinger, shouting for us to
gather around in a circle. "The bullring," he called it. Short but
strong, he never blinked, and we waited for him to call a name
and then another, and once the match was set, we gathered
around the two, pounded our thigh pads twice, and clapped
our hands together, slowly at first, then faster, until the sound
echoed off the brick walls of the school and Coach blew his
whistle and the two in the middle got down in their stances,
and Coach blew the whistle again, and like pit bulls they went
after each other, trying to stand the other up, to get underneath
his pads, raise him off his feet, and drive him into the dirt. Then
Coach selected another challenger to take on the winner, and
we began to pound our pads again, and sometimes the winner
took on four or five of us until he was too tired to win again,
unable to survive the entire team's attack, and we said, "Hoo-
ah!" for his effort, but he received nothing but a drink of water
from the rusted buckets on the sideline, not even Justin, who
took on twenty-three of us at the end of one practice, me
included, but lost his footing when the rain started and rolled
into a chunky second-string tackle, spraining the kid's knee,
causing Coach to issue a penalty for chop blocking, saying, "You
just cost us fifteen yards, Baker!" I can still see Justin standing
there, covered in mud, a divot of dirt and grass stuck in his face
mask, as clearly as I can Coach, whistle between his teeth and
the rain streaming down his Red Raiders windbreaker, the rest
of the team silent, waiting for instruction on what to do next.

The last game of that year we played against the Serpents. They had this beast of a running back with offers from about every Division I school in the country. Despite his scoring three touchdowns in the first half, we were able to keep the score close. Our defense strengthened over the course of the game, and with a minute left, we were down by three on the Serpents' five-yard line, drawing out the clock for one final play. Then Coach, a stalwart traditionalist, surprised us all by calling a trick play, a fumblerooski, a play we had practiced maybe twice since I'd been on varsity. It was fourth down, and we were on the left hash. The obvious play was a pass out to the flat or a pitch to our running back with Justin and me blocking out front. But this was a chance to make history, go undefeated, and take down the mighty Serpents, who were ranked number one in the state. Jamie, our QB, nervously called the play in the huddle. His voice cracked at the *rooski*. It was all up to me: my hands and legs and heart. Jamie snapped the ball and put it on the ground. The running back darted toward the right hash, followed by our offensive line and most of the Serpents, in their sleek black-and-green uniforms. I pulled the other way, picked up the ball, and started toward the end zone. The Serpents' middle linebacker, a mean-looking, spit-spewing fuck, raced after me and threw a forearm up under my chin, knocking me out of bounds right before the goal line. The Serpents ran out on the field pumping their fists in the sky. Mothers threw cardboard hot dog tubs onto the field, and little kids reenacted the now-infamous last play, embellishing how I went down. "A fucking fumblerooski?" one of the fathers shouted as we were walking back to the locker room. I remember Coach in his office while we cleaned out our lockers, sitting there with this kind of grin on his face, like he enjoyed the fact that we lost. But now I think he enjoyed making the call, taking a chance, and even though it didn't work out, he still did it, called a fumblerooski, gave me the opportunity to be a hero, or something like one.

A PHONE rings from somewhere in the living room. I look around but don't see a landline. The ringtone is playing the Velvet Underground's "Sweet Jane." I walk toward the sound and see a corner of the phone underneath one of the couch cushions.

Coach is standing next to me.

"Aren't you going to answer it?" I ask.

"It's not my phone."

"Whose phone is it?"

"My daughter's," he says.

I pick it up and look at the caller ID, a number with an out-of-state area code.

"Leave it," Coach says.

The ringtone stops and I place the phone on the couch, thinking it's time to leave.

Shit's about to get deep.

"They're all wrong numbers," Coach says. "Did you know Toni?"

"She was a few years behind me, wasn't she?"

"I guess that's right. You kids all seemed to be the same age back then."

He picks up the phone, puts it in his pocket, then sits on the couch.

"She was a dancer," he says. "She couldn't stay here and be a dancer, so she went off to New York. I didn't agree with her plans. She was too young, too frivolous. Her mother and I went to visit and she's sitting there on this futon with her leg hanging over the thigh of another girl and they're laughing and kiss-

ing each other on the lips, right in front of us. We couldn't
understand it. We thought, sure, plenty of queers in those musi-
cals, but our daughter? We refused to see her perform, and
once we got back home, I said I couldn't speak to her for a while.
Though by now she was an adult and could make her own
decisions, I just wasn't going to have a bunch of queers sitting
around the tree at Christmas. We went to see Father Macaby
about it, but he didn't have any quality advice. He said that God
loves all creatures. I guess I felt like Macaby was giving me the
runaround about my daughter and what I should do. Then
Toni's mother gave in, went to New York, and stayed a week,
said it was the best time she'd had in twenty years. All of a sudden she was this different person, younger looking, full of
spunk, wanting to go out dancing. She got a tattoo of a hum-
mingbird on the inside of her thigh. I said, 'What the heck is
wrong with you? We can't support this kind of thing. She's our
daughter. We had plans for her.' 'What plans?' she says. 'You
can't predict the future. If you could, you'd be a much more
interesting person.' See, I had always imagined I would retire
and have Toni nearby, married to a man who treated her right
and gave me a couple of grandkids, and Toni's mother and I
would sit out on the porch and watch them run around on the
lawn, and if they were boys—in my mind they were boys—
I'd teach them how to play ball, and those days would be the
best days I'd ever see. I couldn't get over it the way her mother
could. Later that summer, Toni traveled through Europe in a
dance troupe. She sent us letters, in her beautiful handwriting,
with these little drawings of sculptures and cathedrals and
street scenes. I didn't look at any of them until after she was
gone. She was riding one of those motor scooters just outside
of Florence, and I can still see her, gliding along the highway,
hair whipping around her face, that coy little smile, like she

knew something you would never know. A truck carrying a bunch of chickens clipped her wheel and sent her flying down a hillside."

Coach looks at me as if I'm capable of understanding his pain.

What can I do?

So I ask him if he wants a beer or something.

"A beer sounds good," he says.

SOME DAYS are like that.

I'm sitting on the porch with Coach, drinking beer at ten o'clock in the morning. I got this list of clients waiting for their spring cleanups, but the worry of getting to them passes.

We don't talk much at first. We're like two acquaintances that haven't seen each other in a long time. What've you been up to? How's work? How's the house holding up? Have you seen the new cans on that Dwyer girl's mother? It's been hot but not too humid; they say it's going to rain all next week.

One beer after another and I got a nice buzz going. Coach is laughing at his own thoughts, or maybe it's the three kids kicking a can down the street.

"I used to skip school once in a while," Coach says. "I should've skipped more. Those were great days."

"Once in a while, Justin and I would drive to Wareham and get a jug of this misty-looking booze and sit out on the harbor with our heads spinning, coming up with all kinds of plans."

"Boys don't really change that much. But girls do. It blows my mind what they wear around here. I can pretty much see their ass cheeks in those short-shorts; you can't help but notice."

"I hear you, Coach. I mean, I don't have a daughter, but I

can see how it would probably wreck me if I did have a daughter and she was dressed in next to nothing, going out to the Pines with a bunch of gorillas like we used to be."

"You don't have any control over it. If you do end up getting married and having a family, you have to let go of any notion of control."

"I don't feel like I got any control now."

"Somehow it changes. You don't care about what's going on in the world. You don't have time. One day you have long hair and you're listening to Led Zeppelin and talking about revolution and you feel so strong you could eat a box of nails, then the next you're at the barbershop every two weeks and watching what you eat and suddenly you got all these *things* you have to take care of, so you're checking your bank statements every other day, putting money up against your own life in case something happens to you, which you never even thought about when you were young and didn't have all this stuff. I used to feel so light then. Now it's like I got these weights around my ankles."

"You don't look bad for an old guy," I say, trying to bring us up again, "maybe just a little pale. You should get out of the house more."

"You're right. I should get out of the house more. But I get so exhausted."

We went on, sitting there drinking, going back and forth about what it was like when he was a kid and what it was like when I was a kid. And I'll admit that I started to enjoy Coach's company. I had forgotten about the bunnies, or forgiven him, and even smoked one of his cigars, which made me cough and turn green and Coach sat there laughing at me, then smacked my back so hard I felt my spine crack, and I put him in a headlock but he managed to get my free arm and twist it back till it felt like my forearm was about to snap. I was impressed with how strong he was. He could kill me if he wanted.

I'M NOT sure which of us came up with the idea to go for a drive, but somehow it's already dark and we're in my truck, singing "American Girl" at the top of our lungs, Coach beating the top of the cab with his fist. "I love this song," he says. "Wait, pull over here."

"Mrs. Little's house?"

"She used to call me Bug Eyes in school. She'd walk up behind me with her friends and say, 'Stop staring at me, Bug Eyes.'"

Coach stumbles out of the truck and up to the front step, unzips his pants, and takes a piss right there in the open. Once he's finished, he rambles back to the truck and shouts for me to go.

We bull-rush at least a dozen mailboxes along Hingham Street. I hit one post made of marble and mess my shoulder up. One of the mailboxes is in the shape of a sheepdog's head, and Coach is opening and closing the lid, barking for me to take him to Lakeshore. He holds the sheepdog mailbox in his lap. I can barely see the road now that it's dark, and with one head-light out I'm worrying I might get pulled over.

"Don't sweat it," Coach says. "I know all the cops in town."

AT LAKESHORE, you can't see the lake, because the houses are built up so high.

"There was nothing here when I was a kid," Coach says, "just trampled grass and beach. We used to skinny-dip every Friday night."

He tells me to pull up near one of the houses on the lake. I see a For Sale sign just left of the pebbled driveway. I can make out a red front door and columns on the porch and windows in the moonlight beneath the gabled roof.

"What are we doing here, Coach?"

"Can't you read the name on the mailbox?" he says. "This is my house."

He says his wife is gone for the week, and the way he's walking now, sure, confident, I can tell this is something he does on a regular basis when she's out of town.

"She's got someone new living here. I don't know who, but there're some men's toiletries in the bathroom and a gym bag full of extra-large clothes and a couple suits hanging in the closet I know for a fact aren't mine. I stole a pair of his shoes last time I was up here. He's got big, specific-sized feet. Size thirteen and a half, wide. Now when I'm out, I'm looking down at men's feet. She's free to do what she wants. It's just the idea of her with another man. You know too much about someone you've been with for so long, and then you're thinking, wait, is she making that little move with her tongue on him?"

"So you want her to be alone?"

"I don't know, Mac. It's complicated. Everything I don't want to know, I want to know. It's like when you see that booth for the smallest woman in the world at the state fair. You don't really want to see her, but something makes you give the guy at the tent a dollar and all of a sudden you're in there looking down at this poor little creature and it makes you sick to your stomach and you're better off not having gone inside at all because now you have this image of her in your head forever, grim, with big silver teeth, lying in a bed of hay, and you keep asking yourself, What the hell possessed me to go in there? Why couldn't I just walk past the tent?"

"I sometimes do stuff like that because I don't feel good about my own situation. I'll be at the McDonald's and I'm done eating, but I'll sit there and watch that real fat guy with all the pockmarks on his face shuffling around behind the counter, calling out orders in his high-pitched voice, and then I get depressed."

Coach bats off the mailbox at the foot of the drive and sticks the sheepdog's head on the post, but it slumps to the side and is barely hanging on. He walks up the drive and turns over a few big rocks, scratches his head, looks up at the sky, at the silver clouds in the dark, asks me if I know how to pick a lock.

I point to a window on the side left open an inch or so, and Coach pushes it up.

"Go on, get up there," he says.

Coach holds out his cupped hands and I step up and he pushes from underneath and I grab hold of the window ledge, pull myself up, and worm forward in the dark, feeling a soft carpet beneath me. Then Coach gives my feet a shove and I tumble into the room. My knee cracks against something hard.

"Open the front door, Mac," he says.

I get up and find a light switch and look back at the carefully made bed and the throw pillows on top and the framed painting of an empty beach chair and a few floating seagulls against the pink sky of dusk. It smells like lavender, a healthy, middle-aged scent I once smelled on a woman's neck when we were drunk and in my truck and she kept saying she was old enough to be my mother.

My hand runs along the wall of the hallway, toward the dim light left on in the living room, shining a foot ahead of the front door, where through the side windows I see Coach's bug eyes and grape head peering in impatiently.

"Home sweet home," he says when I open the door.

Coach goes through the refrigerator and pulls out bags of deli meat and mustard and nods toward a cabinet, where there's a loaf of bread.

"She's not starving, that's for sure," he says.

I'm thinking, "How did I end up here?" I remember the bunnies and Coach on the doorstep with the gun in his hand and his sad, dirty living room. Now everything's reversed—everything's clean and neat and orderly. There's no water mark in the sink, I notice, and then I puke in it after eating half the sandwich Coach made for me.

I wash my hands and face and slurp a handful of water, gargle and spit. Coach is upstairs. I can hear his heavy footsteps above me. Out the window above the sink, the lake looks like a dark-purple sky. On the inside ledge is a tiny framed poem that reads:

Mommy and Daddy are in the trees
Making sounds like little bees
When they fall down I won't frown
I'll put Band-Aids on their knees

Coach is standing in the hallway with no shirt on, in a pair of tight swimming trunks, the veins on his legs coiled and popping out of his skin.

"Toni wrote that in the second grade," he says. "Let's take a dip."

"I don't know, Coach," I say.

"Don't be such a pussy. It's refreshing."

Near sober from puking my guts out, I'm back to feeling bad about Coach, wanting him to feel good, so I strip down to my boxers and we walk out on the dock and he dives into the lake, hollers out that it's cold, man, it's cold, and I jump in after him and we swim out toward the circle of light shining like a spotlight on just this one place in all the world.

Coach goes underwater, comes up spitting like a seal, his thin hair matted down on the sides of his head. I can see the boyish face he grew up with, his big eyes and tiny ears and plump lips, bobbing in the water like a buoy that's been out here forever.

My body warms up and I'm floating on my back, kicking my feet beneath the surface of the lake, feeling a sense of freedom, of safety, of calm. I turn over and slither below and come up with my ears plugged, squeezing my nose and blowing hard until they pop. I look around for Coach, but he's gone.

I call out, "Coach, Coach," turning around in the water, paddling my hands and feet, until I see his arms flailing, splashing. I swim out and take his heavy body on my shoulder and wade toward the dock. Now it's a matter of lifting him up onto the wooden planks. I ease up onto the dock and dig my hand into the slab of skin on the back of his neck. I've got so much adrenaline that Coach feels almost weightless. I pull him out of the water as easy as a panfish and roll him over onto his back. His eyes are closed and his cheeks puffed out. I can't tell if he's breathing. I tilt his head up and move close to his pudgy lips, pry them open with my fingers, and blow hard into his mouth until he spurts up water and I'm able to ease him over on his side.

He's squirming and coughing, shaking his head like an old dog gone deaf.

Eventually he gets up and stands there on the dock, his belly hanging out over his trunks and this empty look on his face.

"I've been swimming this lake all my life," he says.

I put a towel around his shoulders, but he doesn't move, just stands there shivering, water dripping down his legs.

I help him across the dock to the lawn, where we sit in a couple of Adirondack chairs, where his ex-wife and her XL lover must sit. We're quiet, Coach looking out at the lake that's always been there, before the houses, before us, the wind cool on my skin and the light of dawn slowly blending into the sky.

IN THE deep humid morning, I pull up to the small house in the Heights, and Coach holds out his hand for me to shake it.

"You're all right, Mac," he says.

His not thanking me is a sign of respect, a pact between men. But I know he knows things are different now.

Next day I don't get up till noon. I make a pot of coffee and sit out on the porch, listening to music as I go over the schedule. I got a hell of a lot of jobs to get to, a hell of a lot of angry voice mails.

Another day, and who knows what to expect?

Coach is outside filling the bird feeders. He salutes me. Then he gets out the hose and waters his gazanias. Those beautiful gazanias blazing, unharmed.

NEVER SO SWEET

~~~

MY UNCLE NEVER did a bad thing to anybody, but one day
while he was on his front porch eating an ice-cream cone, two
men pushed him inside, tied his hands and feet, robbed his
house, and shot him in the head. He was in a coma for a week.
I was nine years old, and my father took me to see him that
first Saturday he was in the hospital. I remember his forehead
was wrapped up and someone had placed a straw hat on his
head. On the television mounted to the far wall, a hefty Italian
woman stirred a pot of tomato sauce.

"How can he watch television when he's asleep?" I asked my
father.

We heard the toilet flush and out walked Tutti, my uncle's
girlfriend.

"How's he look?" she said, gesturing to the hat.

"Like a dead farmer," my father said.

"Whoa, I just had déjà vu," Tutti said, her hand at her chest.

"Any news?" my father asked.

"Nothing. Absolutely nothing." She could tell my father was unhappy about the hat. "This is only to keep me entertained. I've been here for hours. I didn't mean anything by it." She took the hat off his head and put it on. She looked pretty.

"What are you two doing this afternoon?" she asked.

"We didn't have anything planned other than to visit the hospital. Maybe we'll go down to the beach for a little while. Right, bud?"

My father patted me on the back.

"I would just love it if I could come with you."

"What if he wakes up?" I said.

"He won't wake up while we're at the beach," Tutti said.

Tutti was from Ottawa. She didn't live with my uncle. At that time, she had a condo in Naples, Florida, provided for her by another lover, a wealthy man who sold Mercedes-Benzes and turned over foreclosed houses. She was in her mid-forties and married to her high school boyfriend, Thomas, who managed a Tim Hortons donut shop. She flew to Canada in the summers and stayed with him for a month or two and then flew to Boston to be with my uncle in his little cottage near the beach in Wequaquet. Her lover in Florida unknowingly paid for everything. With him, Tutti pretended to be one of the top interior decorators in the world. She had phony business cards and a clientele of rich-sounding names like Thurston Bell and Conner Macintosh. I thought she was beautiful, but I didn't really know what beauty was. My mother died when I was three; she was an artist, and her paintings hung in our house. There is one of a cathedral in Mexico that I particularly like and that I have with me still. The cathedral is off to the side of a dirt road. The viewer stands on the road, considering whether or not to enter the cathedral. She died from a brain embolism. My father and I were asleep when it happened. "She died dreaming," my father used to say. In photographs she was still and easy to forget. But Tutti moved. Her breasts bounced. Her skin changed colors. Her hair glowed in sunlight.

On the way to the beach, my father stopped for coffee and bought me an orange juice and a sugared jelly donut. Tutti sat in the backseat, smoking. I had offered her the front seat, but she said she wanted to stretch her legs.

"You're lucky you weren't here when it happened," my father said to her.

"I know it. And the funny part is—well, not funny really but fortunate, for me—is that I had planned on being here last week but your brother called and said he wasn't feeling well and I should wait a few days before I came down. Maybe he knew something was going to happen."

"He ate a bad clam," my father said. "Where are you staying?"

"I'd planned on the cottage, but I guess the cops are still investigating."

"You can stay with us," I said, and glanced at my father.

"That would be perfect. All the motels in this town smell like seafood."

I laughed at this, but I don't know why. Tutti was odd, and back then I laughed at anything that seemed odd. It was a problem. My father had been depressed ever since my mother died, and maybe before. But I was always laughing.

At the beach, Tutti went into the women's restroom carrying an oversize leopard-print bag. My father and I changed into our bathing suits. We waited for Tutti. The sand was hot under my feet. I dug them in where it was cooler. Tutti was wearing a green polka-dot bikini. There were puffs of hair under her arms, a curled line below her navel, and coils around her calves. Her pubic hair webbed out from beneath her bottoms. She caught me staring and winked.

My father seemed impressed. He had always believed in keeping everything natural. As an architect, he melded the tough peninsular landscape with each house he drew up in his specs. We lived in a classic Greek colonial with cherrywood finish and a mahogany deck. In the winter, we heated the house with a wood-burning stove and fireplace. We bathed three times a week to conserve water. When we went to the beach, he never brought towels or chairs or something to read. He swam for about twenty minutes, then lay down so the sand spackled his entire body. I didn't like the feeling and would run along the shore until I was dry, then sit cross-legged watching the seagulls hover above families with picnic lunches.

"You want to play shark, bud?" my father asked me.

"What's shark?" Tutti said.

"Just a game."

"I want to play, too."

We jogged down to the shore. I stopped at the water's edge, choosing to ease myself in. My father dove straight ahead, the oncoming wave a portal from one world to the next. Tutti knelt down and put her palms on top of the water. Then she stood and faced me, lowered her arms behind her head, arched her torso, and sprung into the water. I was last in and farthest away from my father. I swam out to where I couldn't put my feet down and moved my arms as hard as I could, pretending I was a bigger shark or some sea monster sharks feared. My father went under again and breached the surface with his palms pressed together, his fingers forming the frightening fin. In the North Atlantic, human bodies are invisible underwater. I sensed movement, and that's what made the game fun. When my father caught me, he picked me up on his shoulders and flung me back into the water. I crashed awkwardly, never fully prepared, swallowing and spitting seawater. Tutti burst out laughing. My father came for her next. But he treated her capture differently. He picked her up and carried her to the shore, as though he wasn't sure what he had found.

Tutti lay on her stomach and undid the knot on her bikini top. A faint white line ran across her back. Her hair was darker from the water and speckled with sand. She brought it around her shoulder, squeezed it like a wet rag, and flung it back. She put her hands on her upper arms and rested her chin just inside her left shoulder. She looked at us.

"This is all I've ever wanted from life," she said.

My father gave me a dollar to buy some candy at the snack bar. Full of sugar, I went off to play Wiffle ball with a group of boys near the volleyball nets. The sky was clear. There was a slight breeze. I could see everything.

Later, we lingered at the edge of the shore, silent, listening. There is a time when everyone begins to depart from the beach, as though the beach itself urges them to go, casts them out gently in the falling light, so it can be alone. Then the beach becomes a different place altogether. You can hear the water as well as the internal rhythms of the body. The sun moves downward on an arc. The moon, a phantom, appears.

We drove back to the hospital. This time, Tutti sat up front. I rolled down the window and put my hand out, let the wind push it back. The inside of the car smelled like the sea.

The sheets under my uncle's body were whiter than before. Tutti kissed his cheek.

"They'll trim his beard for him, won't they?" she asked my father.

"I'm sure."

"To be alive and not know it," she said.

We sat in the room until visiting hours were over. Tutti ripped a page out of a magazine and showed me how to make a swan. My father sat near the window with one leg crossed over the other.

The rain started that night and carried into the next day. Tutti and my father stayed up late and played cards and smoked pot. Later, she read his palms.

"All the pain in your life has passed," she said. "See where these lines cross at the bottom? They never cross again."

"Maybe it's the other way around," my father said.

"No. We don't care so much about pain when we're old."

"Do me," I said.

She held my hand in hers and turned it slowly. I felt it was something separate from my body. She had long fingernails, pointed at the tips. She traced the lines in my palm with the end of her ring finger.

"Yours is different than your father's," she said. She seemed concerned. I started to take my hand away. "No, it's okay. Your lines branch out into these three paths. I think it means there will be three distinct periods in your life. Now you are young and learning. Later you will be successful and have a lovely wife and healthy children. Then you will live comfortably, even if the world is falling apart all around you in your old age."

"Sounds horrifying," my father said.

"Oh, don't," Tutti said.

"I mean, we all need to suffer a little. You don't want to fill his head with this idea that there won't be any pain in his life." He turned to me. "Bad things will happen. They have to. They're good for you, anyway."

Then he told me to get some sleep. My father let Tutti have his bed. He said he would sleep on the couch.

In the summer, there was no limit on how much time I could spend awake. I tried to fold a piece of paper into a swan like Tutti had showed me. I arranged my music cassettes in alphabetical order. I went under the bed and imagined what it would be like to be buried alive. I entertained the Wimbles and the Wobbles, two factions of planetary warriors, who, in their battle for universal domination, found themselves floating aimlessly in the ether, waiting for me to decide their fates.

Then I heard the bed in my father's room creaking. My father had fits of restlessness and bad dreams. His doctor had given him pills to help him sleep, and it'd been a while since I'd heard any noise from his room during the night. I went out to the living room and saw that the blanket was spread open on the couch and my father was not there. I heard Tutti moan and the bed creak. Then I heard my father get up and use the bathroom.

THE NEXT day, my uncle died. It happened early that morning. A series of muffled cries from the living room reached me in my sleep and, like a remnant from a dream, a sort of soft rain, I woke and went downstairs to find Tutti with her head on my father's knee. She seemed smaller than before, like a sister only a few years older than me. My father stared straight ahead, an arm across her shoulders, as though he were driving somewhere.

Later that afternoon, I heard Tutti on the phone in the kitchen. She was whispering, but her voice was so high-pitched that even a whisper was sharp and clear.

"You didn't have anything to do with this, did you?" she said.

"He was harmless. It was all me. I don't know why I do these things."

I could hear her whimpering now. I peeked out and saw her sitting on a stool at the kitchen counter, her shoulders slumped forward, her face cocked to the side with her left hand hovering over the receiver.

"I do love you. . . . No I don't think you're a fool. . . . Oh, God."

My legs were trembling; whatever was in my gut had poured down into them.

My father entered the kitchen from the sunroom, where he often read in the late afternoon.

Quickly, Tutti's voice changed. "Oh, yes, yes, it's been beautiful here, Mother."

I watched my father give Tutti a kiss on the forehead. She covered the receiver.

"I'll only be another minute."

"Don't be a snoop," my father said, and pinched my nose as he passed by on his way into the living room.

I KEPT quiet about what I'd heard. I felt sick, the kind of sick you feel right before you're about to puke. I went with my father to the funeral home and to the places he had in mind to spread his brother's ashes. They had a sister living in Amsterdam, who my father kept trying to reach. He hadn't spoken to her in ten years.

I didn't know my uncle very well. I really didn't know anyone at that age, and only now when I look back have I come to the conclusion that the entire history of my family is a sort of fiction, misunderstood by me alone. According to my father, my uncle was a spiritual man. Whether people thought he was a peacenik or hippie didn't matter. He'd been touched, as they say, by some kind of light. That's what I remember about him. His eyes glowed in the same way a woman's does the moment before they begin to well up.

"I missed the lottery, but your uncle didn't," my father said.

We were driving to collect my uncle's ashes. Tutti was with us. I tried not to look at her, but it was impossible; I kept seeing her even when I closed my eyes.

"Lucky for him," my father went on, "he was a terrible shot. He was sent to Germany, where he worked as a transition agent for soldiers heading back to the world, as they called it then. No one liked him very much until he started dealing hash. He used to hollow out Roman candles and stuff it in the center so the dogs couldn't smell it. But one night he got busted crossing the French border. 'Too many candles for a grown man,' the officer said. He was discharged.

"When he returned, he had all these ideas about the cosmos. He said that this life he'd been living was just one of many lives and that he no longer feared death, because this was only one part of him, and there were other parts out in the universe that he had yet to experience. Maybe I'm not explaining it well. What I remember is that he was sincere about these other lives he was living. Mirror lives, he called them."

"So like different versions of ourselves?" I asked.

"That's exactly right," Tutti said, her voice a pinprick in my ear.

"When I think about it," my father said, "he never worried about anything. Sometimes that infuriated me and sometimes it made me envious."

We were heading out to Chatham, on Cape Cod, a town that looks the same now as it did then and as it did when my father was a boy: cottages scattered along the coast, an old-style pump-handle gas station, seafood shacks, and cluttered used-book stores.

"I think he would've liked to have his ashes spread out here. This way, the ocean can take him in all different directions."

Tutti put her head in her hands and began to cry. My father looked at me somberly. I didn't feel scared. It was something else, something I recognized a few years later. That was the first and only time I ever pitied him.

THE MEN who shot my uncle came from Fall River. They were brothers in their mid-thirties, failed fishermen who, like many in those decaying towns along the Eastern Seaboard, had been relegated to car-repair work or boat cleaning but, shunning that sort of labor, took to robbing houses in the alcoves where a handful of wealthy holdovers from a once-prosperous time still lived. Their name was Bodfish. They'd both spent time in prison but not for the same crimes. Carey, the older brother, did five years in Walpole for auto theft, and Stephen did fifteen months in Dedham for unarmed robbery. It wasn't clear when the two decided to become killers. It was Carey Bodfish who'd fired the gun.

Either way, they weren't very good at killing, or stealing. They left their fingerprints all over the cottage, and one of the brothers had used the toilet, forgetting to flush. With their profiles already on record, police raided their vacated apartment, discovering some of the stolen goods my father had reported missing: a twelve-speed mountain bike, my grandfather's stamp collection, a bronzed statue of Miles Davis, a Les Paul electric guitar, and a worthless reproduction of a Mayan mask that, nevertheless, meant a great deal to my uncle because he'd watched a man in Morelia create it from a block of wood. Except for the stamps, which my father kept in a safe-deposit box in case we ever needed to sell them, the rest of my uncle's things were stored in the garage, still sealed as evidence. Years later, when I graduated from college, he asked if I wanted anything from the house for my apartment in Boston, and I took the mask and the statue of Miles Davis and the electric guitar, though I never learned to play.

The Bodfish brothers were mean-looking black-eyed Irishmen. All through the investigation, trial, and sentencing, they didn't mention any names. They were given life in prison without parole. In the papers they were known as *The Statue Brothers*, because their faces never changed in the courtroom. If you still read the paper closely, which I tend to do, you might've seen a brief blurb in the Metro section of the *Globe* about Carey Bodfish dying of lymphoma. He was fifty-seven years old, the same age my father was when he passed away three months ago.

"I WANT you to know everything," Tutti said on the night of my father's wake, twenty years after my uncle died, in the unusual dark of a June evening. "I mean, none of it really makes sense. You start trying to tell your life story and you realize how random it all is. That's why I don't like novels or movies. Everything's so neatly condensed. But, still, I think it's important you know the truth."

Those next few weeks after we spread my uncle's ashes, Tutti stayed with us. She went shopping and made big, hearty meals of meat and potato stew, steak tips, and baked cod. She claimed her cooking acumen from growing up as the child of a single father. Her mother had been a professor of Eastern religions and fell in love with a graduate student from Ghana.

The two ran off together and left Tutti and her father alone. Soon they moved out to the countryside, to a decaying farmhouse where her father's grandparents had once lived. Her father got the farm running again and bought two cows and a dozen hens. Tutti learned to cook. She enjoyed watching her father eat.

I SPENT the rest of that summer out of the house. Sometimes I'd hook up with Ryan or Sean and we'd talk about stealing candy from the store on Southbay or make like we were trying to break the windows of the old Tradewinds Hotel. One day I threw a rock as hard as I could, which was a no-no because we had an unspoken agreement that we weren't actually going to commit crimes, only talk about committing them, and Ryan and Sean took off, and an alarm sounded, and I ran in the other direction. Ryan and Sean didn't come to the meeting spot anymore, and I was alone.

Sometimes I'd cruise on my bike along the coastal trails that wound past Wequaquet Harbor into the port and up the cliffside properties where rich folks posted No TRESPASSING signs along the street, and reflected in whose wide, floor-length windows I could see what they saw as they drank their morning coffee: the fog low and thick above the ocean, the fishing boats easing through the gray. I climbed the hill to the country club, where I collected golf balls in the gullies and marshes and resold them outside the club's entrance for a quarter apiece. Later, I swam in the ocean and sat under the Wequaquet Bridge with a chicken salad sandwich, watching the silver-bellied fish shoot up from the river. I rode to the gas station and put air in my tires. In the insect hum of noon, I playacted tragic death scenes in the swampland behind the Taylors' burned-out house.

Covered in filth, eaten by mosquitoes, tired and wet and hungry, I returned home, washed in the tub, and ate at the table with my father and Tutti, who by then had begun to love and care for each other. In the soft laughter that followed an unintentional burp, the playful smack on the hand when my father attempted to serve himself, the way they spoke each other's names like cherished objects, I became invisible and so further penetrated the fantastical and unexplainable worlds that hung in my brain.

A month or so after my uncle's murder, during a night when I had been so lost in a struggle between the Wimbles and the Wobbles, I was struck by the greatest fear I'd ever known, the fear that there is nothing beyond the universe. That we were contained by an infinite darkness was inconceivable to me, and this single, piercing thought caused me to break out in a fit of screams.

Though I remember screaming, I don't remember how long I went on for, as is the case when, on occasion, I find myself in the kitchen or living room, suddenly overwhelmed by a flash of white, a thought, a memory of a voice or smell I realize I have missed for so long. Only now it is my wife who comes to me and holds me and kisses my neck and cheek and takes my hand in hers and sits by my side until I'm spent, relieved of whatever force has overtaken me. If ever I was scared when I was a boy, my father would turn on a light and sit beside me reading a book until I fell back asleep. That night, though, it was Tutti who came to my room.

I was sitting up in bed with my head between my knees. She switched on the bedside lamp and sat down. She was a little drunk, I could tell, smiling at me, at my eyes peeking out at her.

"It's just me," she said, and laughed brightly, her eyes sparkling in the soft lamplight.

I was nervous with her so close, as if I knew what she was really capable of. But I was also tired and afraid of something bigger than the two of us, and I acquiesced to her easy voice and gentle smile.

She took my head in her hands and brought it out of the small hole I had created between my knees, as an archaeologist might lift a petrified skull from the earth, guiding me toward the pillow, not wanting to shake up any more of the thoughts in my head.

Tutti lay down beside me and turned her head. Her breath smelled of wine and cigarettes and cake, a silent midnight snack saved from that night when she and my father had gone to Alberto's to give her a break from cooking. I felt the warmth of her palm hovering an inch above my chest. Her fingers drifted back and forth like wheatgrass.

"I want you to say these things with me," she said, her voice unchanging. "First, I'll go. Then you repeat what I've said. Okay?"

I nodded. Sweat gathered in a shallow pool at the base of my neck.

"I am not a boy," she said.

I was silent. I didn't understand.

"Say it, sweetie. You'll feel better. Think of this as a departure from yourself." She repeated, "I am not a boy."

"I am not a boy," I said quietly, somewhat embarrassed.

"I am not a son."

"I am not a son."

"Good," she said, continuing to draw her fingers in a gentle swoosh down the middle of my chest. "Relax, now. Listen to your voice.

"I live nowhere."

"I live nowhere."

"I want nothing."

"I want nothing."

"I need nothing."

"I need nothing."

"I am never awake or asleep."

"I am never awake or asleep."

"I have no eyes, no ears, no mouth, no body."

"I have no eyes, no ears, no mouth, no body."

"I am nothing I know."

"I am nothing I know."

"I am an unchanging, eternal being."

"I am an unchanging, eternal being."

"I was never born, and I will never die."

"I was never born, and I will never die."

It seemed like listening and repeating what I had heard did more to soothe me than what was actually said.

MY FATHER did seem happier, though I believe it had more to do with not being alone than with Tutti's mantras and meditations. He would jog in the mornings, stretching beforehand in the kitchen, a sweatband tight around his head guarding the thin black curls of his hair. He exhaled in quick bursts just before darting out the door. I remember the smell of new sweat, the stain on his shirtfront like some kind of godhead, and the veins along his arms uprooted as he drank a large glass of water.

That fall, I began middle school. I would leave the house early and ride my bike past the river and up a long, winding hill that opened onto a pleasant street with small cottages guarded by looming maple trees, then through the cemetery where my mother was buried, wondering, How is it where you are? Past Big Tim's Auto Emporium and down Isaac Road, where children in buses screamed to me from the windows en route to that hideous, flat Y-shaped building that was Wequaquet Middle. With the exception of my desire to see the young teaching assistant in my social sciences class, Ms. Cone, naked, nothing from the time spent there has stayed with me.

But at home I was beginning to learn how love can be born from violence and misery and odd circumstances. Tutti had left for a weekend. As my father and I played cribbage in the kitchen, a sudden uproar of chirping birds caused his hand to tremble over the board. I can believe now that Tutti possessed a certain power over men, as the greatest women often do, that when that power takes hold we are no longer controlled by our pasts, the places in which we live, the people we know or have known, or the public spectacle of sport and politics, which at that time consisted mainly of disarming and killing a mustachioed man in a beret, from a country whose name sounded like a deathly cough. Tutti consumed my father. I understood that a woman could do this to a man, could strip away all misfortune and pain, leaving us even more naked and vulnerable.

When she returned, Tutti brought with her two large suitcases full of clothes, a dozen books on New Age spirituality, certain childhood possessions she felt she could not live without, and word that she had finally divorced Thomas, who, in a vain attempt to rekindle their marriage, had brought Tutti to a ski resort outside Montreal.

The Wimbles and Wobbles had signed a ceasefire and I was bored. I sat at the top of the stairs and listened to Tutti explain herself.

"I let him make love to me," I heard her say. "But then, halfway through it, he stopped and said, 'It's over, isn't it?' He could tell by the way my body felt. Then he cried. All night he cried. I went out and hiked up to the empty ski lifts and sat in one of the chairs for so long I fell asleep. A woman from the hotel woke me and said it was going to get cold and they didn't want to be liable if I were to get sick. When I went back to the room, Thomas was gone. He'd packed and left and put some money on the dresser as though I were a prostitute. I guess I deserved to feel that way, but I only felt sad for him. I want good things for Thomas. He loved me."

The three of us had slowly acclimated to the unusual trajectories that had brought us together. My uncle's death seemed so long ago. We believed we were a family, that whatever was past was past, and moving forward through each small yet significant change to the house's interior—the kitchen painted red, the living room rearranged, the dusty trinkets my mother had collected boxed away and replaced with thick, clean-smelling candles—we became comfortable with the rituals of life that included Tutti. She made lunch for me on weekday mornings, set a wonderful spread for Thanksgiving and Christmas, and, because I grew three inches that year, took me to the Atrium in Braintree and bought me new clothes.

We weren't without our struggles, though. This was during the last housing crunch, and my father's company hadn't sold a new home since the summer. Local businesses were yielding to corporate buyouts, and Wequaquet began to resemble the thousands of towns and suburbs across the country unable to hold out through the crisis. Electronics stores and clothing outlets and fast-food joints I had only seen in the city were popping up all over our small town.

Seagulls perch on the gabled entrances, swooping down to peck at the strewn garbage in the sandy parking lots. But this is the present, on a sad, beguiling drive through my old town, kids dicking around in their W-printed letter jackets, with no sense of the future, as we pass MegaWorld on our way toward the beachfront, unchanged and drenched in sunlight; my wife in her retro green one-piece bathing suit; we, like any other tourists, down for Labor Day weekend, lying on the same beach under the same sky listening to the same waves my father and mother and childhood self once did. I can see them in the pockets of unclaimed sand.

THROUGH THE spring and into the following summer, my father was out of work. He picked up odd jobs. He mowed lawns, built decks, and repainted some of the houses he had designed. When I was off from school, I worked with him. I cannot remember a time when I felt as comfortable with my father: his big, callused hands holding me up from the ladder so that I could sweep out the gutters; stripping and priming and painting the long wooden fence along Farm Acres Road; spreading the thick, sour-smelling mulch around the shrubs and flower beds of those large houses on the water; and in the cool summer afternoon, listening to sports radio, packing up our tools, and coiling the extension cords, the sweat dried into our shirts, stinking and spent but alive, sensing the tightening of the muscles in my forearms and chest, and the windows rolled down on the ride home, listening to the air rush by, the sun an orange disc descending over the town, light moving through us, giving way to night.

I recall feeling present, without worry, free. But I'm not sure that was the case. Or maybe it's that I've lived awhile now and have never been able to get back to that feeling. Or it could be that my memory has tricked me into believing that at one time I lived between the drastic highs and lows that come with each passing day. Sometimes I feel so overjoyed I could break down in tears, so enraged I could smash my fist through a window.

My tendons and muscles and nerves stretch tight as newly strung guitar strings, until somebody, dead or alive, plucks an off chord, sending a shiver throughout my body.

Last February, I lost a tooth in a fistfight outside a bar. I wasn't very drunk. There was just something about the place, the music, the people—this sense of dread and fatigue, a general apathy to the living world—and without provocation I decked a sorry-looking man who was sitting by himself in the barroom corner. We were thrown out onto the street and a crowd gathered. The man was a quick and thoughtful fighter. I must have swung low and mistakenly brought my body forward, exposing the right side of my face, which he struck with the hammer-like bone of his elbow, sending an expensively crowned molar flying into the snow. How pathetic it was to be searching out there in the unplowed street for my tooth. Though, as I dug my hands into the soft, cold powder, I felt something close to that sense of freedom I knew when I was a boy.

MAYBE IT'S because that time in my life was so short and strange that I think about it often. I dress Tutti in short-shorts and a tight-fitting top and my father in worn khakis and a polo shirt. We eat fried seafood out on the boat at Baxter's Landing, throw French fries to the seagulls, and watch the schooners and sailboats drift in the harbor. My father has his arm around Tutti's waist, her head on his shoulder, and we stand by as the old Chevrolets file down Main Street, drivers honking their horns, repositioning the small, newly washed mirrors as their passengers wave to us.

When we returned home from one of these late-summer afternoons, there was a cream-colored Mercedes parked in the driveway. Tutti grabbed hold of my father's arm and steered the car away from the house. "Keep driving! Keep driving!" she shouted. "Please!" My father braked and the engine stuttered; then, with a shot of gas, the car burst ahead.

When you're a kid, a year can feel as long as a decade, and I had mostly forgotten about the man from Florida, what I imagined to be his role in my uncle's death, even the guilt I had felt so strongly after hearing Tutti speak to him on the phone. But it all came rushing back to me then.

What my father said then was, "Oh, fuck this," but what he was really saying was something along the lines of, I knew nothing could be so good. And even before we went back to the house, he had given up on Tutti.

"What are you doing?" Tutti shouted. "Are you crazy or something?"

"That's my house. If someone's in there, then I'm going to throw him out."

"He has guns," Tutti said, her voice lowering, but not enough to keep me from hearing.

"Well if he wanted to kill you, he would've done it a long time ago. Now, if he's come for me, at least there'll be witnesses."

It was instantly clear what was going on.

My father's view of his own mortality put me over the edge. I felt as though I were calling out to him from the bottom of a well. "Please, Dad, listen to her."

"Don't worry, bud," he said with certainty. "We'll be fine."

I heard everything as my father approached the front door. Summer afternoons have an eerie music about them, of swarming insects, water seeping from the bottoms of exposed air conditioners, the buzz of charging electricity through hanging telephone wires. He guarded himself by pulling his left arm across his chest and lowering his shoulder, as though he were drawing a cape over his body, as though he were the assailant, set to unmask himself to an unassuming victim. And although I was afraid, what good did meditation do any of us at that moment? We could not detach from our bodies.

Tutti ran after my father. I jumped out of the car and cowered near the front tire. When my father entered the house, my legs went numb and my face burned hot. I crept up to the door and swiftly moved inside, looking left and right; nothing had been damaged. The house was filled with the foreign scent of strong cologne.

My father was standing by the bathroom door in the hallway. Tutti, opposite him, saw me and put her finger to her lips. The toilet flushed and the man inside the bathroom coughed wickedly, cropping up a wad of phlegm from his throat.

"By God," the man said, and opened the door.

My father struck him in the side of the head and the man stumbled sideways into Tutti's arms. Tutti tried to hold him up, but his weight was in his belly and he slipped from her arms. My father had split some kind of polyp on the man's earlobe, and the blood was streaming down his neck. His eyes were closed and his left arm was stretched out, flailing like a fish on a dock.

"He's an old man," Tutti said. "You didn't have to hit him like that."

"He'll be fine," my father said. "Don't you think he'll be fine?" He bent down and looked at the man, turned and stared at me with eyes still wide, buzzing from the thrill of sudden violence.

"Oh, poor Rudy," Tutti said.

"Poor Rudy?" my father cried. "The man broke into my house. And Rudy? Rudy and Tutti? What a pair!"

Stroking Rudy's face, Tutti asked me to go to the kitchen and pour him a glass of water. I could hear her and my father arguing: She wanted to get Rudy to a hospital, and my father refused, saying he was going to call the police. I hoped for Rudy to wake up. Adults in vulnerable positions made me nervous. This is why children cannot stand to see their parents asleep.

I returned with the water and handed it to Tutti. She had Rudy propped up in her lap now. His eyelids rose slightly and Tutti put the glass to his lips.

"Drink this," she said.

As he drank, he began to cough, and the water shot from his mouth and dribbled down his chin.

"Ah!" he cried.

"Help him up," Tutti said to my father.

"Christ almighty," my father said, and put his arms up under Rudy's shoulders and pulled him to his feet. He slung Rudy's arm over his neck and brought him to the couch. Tutti fluffed up a pillow, and together they laid Rudy down.

Except for the bloodied ear, he was a good-looking older man. He had straight, strawberry-blond hair combed neatly away from his brow and stuck in this position by some kind of mousse—none of it moved from the punch or the fall. He was wearing blue khaki shorts and an expensive-looking yellow shirt. His limbs were weirdly thin in comparison to his hard, curved belly. There was a scar along his left knee, and his legs were strikingly hairless. His belt had tiny sailboats printed on it.

Tutti sat beside him with a towel and a bowl of water. She dampened the towel and cleaned the dried blood away from his ear and neck.

My father stood above us all, looking down as though assessing a sorry litter of dogs he very well knew no one was going to want.

"Okay, then. What's this all about?" he said.

Tutti put the end of the towel in the bowl. The water turned a cloudy red.

"I was sitting out there for a while, hoping to see Tutti, and then I just figured I'd try the door because I drove all the way here and it seemed childish to wait in the car. The door was open. How wonderfully secure you all feel in these old New England towns. This is quite a place. I can see Tutti's influence."

"Right. Right. We live together. How's that affect you?"

"I love her. I've loved her for a long time now, and I don't think it's a mystery that I need someone to take care of me."

"Is that what love is?" my father said, pacing. "Caretaking? Is that what you want, Tutti? You want to make his meals and take him for walks and wipe his ass?"

"Not in front of him," Tutti said, nodding toward me. Her voice was steady and confident. She lived to make momentous choices.

"Listen, baby," Rudy said. "I'm not doing too well. I've got a tumor in my noggin. They say it could be anywhere from three months to a year, but that's with treatment. I don't want to spend the rest of my life in a hospital bed. I'm going out on the boat. I'm sailing to Cape Town. People have always told me it's the most beautiful place on earth, and if I make it there, well, what better place to die in than the most beautiful one? So, what I'm asking is, will you come with me?"

My father and I waited for Tutti to answer, mystified by this man's brashness.

Tutti looked at my father, who stood now with his arms across his chest, then back to Rudy. We were all boys, all the same to her, all wanting and waiting. My father and Rudy were as silent as closed doors, which, if opened, would unveil to her an entirely new life.

"Can't we talk about this in the morning?" she said. "I need some time to think."

"And what do we do with him?" my father said.

"We can't just kick him out now."

My father ran his hand through his hair. His eye twitched. You could tell he didn't want to be so decent.

THAT NIGHT, no one but Rudy slept. Tutti stayed in the bedroom, while my father read in the kitchen. I sat in my room with the lights on and finally went downstairs when I sensed the uneasiness throughout the house.

I took the cribbage board out and asked my father if he wanted to play.

"Not tonight, bud," he said, and went back to looking at the real estate section of the paper. His eyes weren't moving.

Later that night, the Wimbles broke the ceasefire and advanced fearlessly toward the barricade set up by the Wobbles, blasting away the walls with advanced weaponry. During their last intergalactic battle, the Great Leaders of both factions met face-to-face on a distant planet, where they could see the fighting millions of light-years away. First they dined and reflected on what had brought them to this point. Then, understanding that any sort of peace was futile, they had their servants dress them in the dated garb of earthly soldiers, drew their swords, and, with a fateful nod, positioned themselves for a final battle. As they approached each other, I heard Tutti sobbing in the bedroom.

"Oh, I have to," she cried.

And my father's voice: "No, you don't. Don't you see that you have a good thing here? You're going to throw it all away if you leave."

"But imagine if—"

"No," my father shouted. "Don't bring my wife into this."

"But just imagine."

I went downstairs and into the living room. Rudy was still asleep on the couch. I touched his face lightly, feeling the sharp edges of his unshaved chin. His eyes opened and he grabbed my wrist.

"Who are you?" he said.

I whacked him in the mouth with my free hand. He moaned and sneezed and, sitting up, called for Tutti through his hands with a muffled cry.

"I knew it was a bad idea to have him here," my father said, coming up behind me.

"What did you do, sweetie?" Tutti said to me. I realized that I was standing there with my hand still bunched up in a fist.

Tutti inspected his lip and cradled the old man's head in her arms.

"We have to go," she said, and helped Rudy to his feet.

For the first time she looked like an ugly woman to me.

My father had a faint smile on his face. I had imparted a kind of justice for him, yet I didn't feel good about what I had done. I felt that I had to do something more. I had to tell my father what I knew, that Rudy was responsible for sending those men to my uncle's house and that Tutti knew all about it. But I couldn't spit it out. Rudy looked so harmless, so bewildered and broken, that to turn him in seemed like it would only make everything worse.

MY FATHER never saw Tutti again. Until he got sick, he refused to speak about her or to even have her name mentioned in the house. He dated a few women here and there and, just before I left for college, asked one of them, a customs agent at Logan, who was older than him by ten years and carried a gun, if she'd like to move in. He called her his companion. I doubt he loved her, but she cared for him during the remainder of his life, and as my own life began to take shape, I was comforted knowing he was not alone.

When I stayed with him this summer, playing cribbage on the sun porch in the late-evening light, he recounted everything he could remember, leaping from one point in time to the next, from one life to another. He was lucid and free of anger, and he told me about my uncle and about Tutti and the man from Florida, and he also described my mother, how beautiful she was, how much he missed her. What made him so depressed during that time before Tutti was how angry he felt at her dying.

"But it wasn't her fault," he said. "It was just some freak thing that happened."

He wanted me to know he thought most of life was like this: that there are no coincidences, that our lives are strange and never work out the way we think they should.

"And it's all right," he said. "It's better this way."

But then he said, "I can't believe I'm dying. I really can't believe it."

I was with him that night in the hospital. He began gasping for air, and with each attempt at breathing, his body expanded and crumpled. His eyes were so big and his left eye was looking right at me, while his other was rolled back, as though warning me that he was up ahead, close to the other side, and he couldn't see anything yet.

TUTTI SHOWED up at my father's wake alone. She'd cut her hair short and put on ten pounds or so. She had dark circles under her eyes from crying, but she held herself together and gave me a hug and kneeled at my father's casket, making whatever amends she needed to make.

Later, my wife and I were standing outside, waiting for the remaining mourners to leave.

"This is such a stupid ritual," my wife said.

"I guess it's the same as when you're born. Everyone wants to have a look at you and they have no idea what your life is going to be like, so they just look, and when you're dead, they look at you the same way."

A string of fireworks was set off across the road. It was the week before the Fourth of July, and people were already celebrating.

"You were good to have stayed with him all that time," my wife said. She stroked my neck with her long, thin fingers and went back into the funeral home.

I went to the car to get the air conditioner running. Parked beside me was the old cream-colored Mercedes I remembered from so many years ago. New Mexico plates were fixed to the rusted-out bumper. A thin line of smoke escaped from the lowered driver's-side window. I went around to the passenger-side door and looked in. The backseat was piled high with clothes and shoes and bags and one of the flower arrangements from the wake. I tapped my knuckle on the window. Startled, Tutti dropped her cigarette between her boots and hurried to pick it up and stamp it out in the ashtray. She motioned for me to get in the car.

"Oh, my God," she said. "You're so grown up now. It's unbelievable. And I know what they were telling you in there, but you look nothing like your father. I don't even see a resemblance. Well, maybe your nose."

"You're living in New Mexico now?"

"I did for a little while. Santa Fe. It's a wonderful city. Clean. And everyone has so much energy. But I missed the water."

"So, are you in Florida?"

"No. That's a state I'd be happy never to see again."

"My wife and I were down in Miami for a week last year. I thought I saw you in Lincoln Square, but it was someone else."

I had followed the woman, whoever she was, to this little dress shop on a corner. I saw her through the glass window: a plain-looking woman shuffling through short tropical dresses on a rack, the same age Tutti was back when I knew her.

"It's all so phony. And you have to be rich. I guess you can tell that I'm not rich, and hopefully you don't think I'm phony."

"I never did."

"What, then? I mean, what *did* you think?"

"I thought you loved my father. But I also thought that you couldn't change who you were. I know he loved you, and I know that when you left, he wasn't ever as happy again."

"Me, neither," Tutti said. She lit another cigarette and blew the smoke out in patchy clouds, coughing a bit, waving a mosquito from her face. "But I wasn't used to being so comfortable. It scared me, you know? There wasn't anything to be afraid of, but that's what was so frightening. I did try to come back after Rudy died. I called your father and I even flew up here to see him, but he wouldn't talk to me. He was a hard man. Forgiveness is for suckers, anyway. I wouldn't forgive me. That made things easier. Has made things easier. Because now I'm thinking, What would it have been like if I'd stayed? Would I be any different? You know, inside? Probably not. But everything else would be. The outside, I mean."

We were silent for a while. Tutti put out her cigarette, smiled at me, and lowered her head. The last of the people who'd come to see my father started up their cars and drove off. My wife was standing by the door, talking to my father's companion and Mr. Simmons, the funeral director. The light in the parking lot went out. We were two dark figures in a car.

"A whole bunch of other stuff has happened to you, right?" Tutti said then. "It's not just this? I mean, your father and me, we're not everything. We're just a part of the thing. You have a beautiful wife and I'm sure you'll have lovely children, and whatever else is going to happen won't have much to do with the past, I don't think."

How easily I asked her then, thinking that I might never get another chance, if it was true that Rudy had my uncle murdered.

I don't believe she intended to laugh, but that's what she did. I was exhausted in my grief and maybe accepted her apology too easily.

"No," she said. "Two maniacs zonked out of their minds killed your uncle. But when I told Rudy, he had me believe he was responsible, that he had that kind of power. He knew he was losing me; he could hear it in my voice. He must've thought that if I feared him enough, I'd come back, which, as you know, I did. But not because of your uncle."

Tutti raised her head and sneezed three times, a high-pitched, awful-sounding sneeze.

"Bless you," I said.

"Thanks, sweetie," she said, and blew her nose into a napkin. "You don't think I'm a bad person, do you?"

"No," I said. "I don't think that."

★　★　★

I COULDN'T sleep that night. My wife stayed up with me, and we watched television and ate grilled cheese and talked about what I don't remember. It felt like one of those nights in college when she and I lay in bed and told each other about everything we knew, all those stories, so we could stay awake and not be away from each other.

At dawn, we showered together. My wife looked beautiful in the pink light. Her skin was slightly tanned, with tiny freckles on her shoulders. She felt soft against my body. Her hair smelled like something tropical. We made love and lay in bed with the ceiling fan whirring above us.

She'd heard most of what there was to tell about Tutti and my father and my uncle's murder. What I never told her before was that small detail I began this story with, that my uncle was eating an ice-cream cone when the Bodfish brothers attacked him. That, before the lights went dark, the last thing he tasted was something sweet.

She responded in her yawning, half-asleep voice, "How would you know that?"

It was a good question.

How did I know?

BALLAD

～～～～～

OKAY SHE'S GONE let's get set up amp cord guitar now this is romantic this is a gift D C G yep way out of tune needs a good tuning can't remember how to tune just listen listen it all makes sense if you just listen that's what Miles Davis once said I think maybe it was Mingus turn the keys thumb the E and A and okay we're in tune music first then lyrics a mix of dark and light of high and low nothing too dark nothing too light it's her birthday she doesn't want a slit-your-wrists song and she doesn't want some loopy gumball sing-along a ballad of course ballad in D too light ballad in E minor too dark ballad in C C to F to D C to F to G something's missing C to F to A minor to G that's it that makes sense there's a balance there okay C to F to A minor to G for a while and squawking squawking why are you upset buddy why are you hiccuping now and that cute-as-hell laugh can't miss that laugh got to take a picture if I time it right though you never do it when I got the phone pointed at you guitar rest

camera phone on hiccup and you're looking at me like I'm some
creature from Mars wide-eyed scared shitless considering the
size of your world for the past ten minutes little stuffed mon-
keys and parrots and lizards and then this giant indigenous
freak from across the river comes stomping through the bush
into your perfectly unreal world wanting to strip it bare take
you away turn it into a resort which think about it little buddy
think about living your first couple years in a beautiful resort
no bugs or scary animals just people like your mother all there
to serve you while you relax under an umbrella with the sun
on your little toes doesn't that sound nice sound like something
you could appreciate later on in life if say you were to make a
bunch of money and then lose a bunch of money at the point
your future wife is five months pregnant surprise and already
has you in a convertible crib on credit without considering the
possibility that maybe we won't have the money that we'll never
have the kind of money we had then and we moved all the studio equipment into the garage where Mommy says it should
be anyway considering I haven't recorded a thing since we
moved back to her hometown from L.A. fifteen years ago and
what was that just a little number called "I Do and I Don't" just
a song that put her in the cream-colored Mercedes she rides into
Boston to have lunch with Karen and Odessa and Hilary like
they're the goddamn New England version of *Sex and the City*
like they're impressed by my fifteen-year-old Benz she says I
have to take the train in from Haverhill for Christ's sake well
at least you have a car and you're not some poor Mexican walking to work along Route 1 okay okay no sad-time Daddy talk I
get it come here get rid of those hiccups okay I didn't mean to
bring you down let's go out to the living room and you can help
with Mommy's birthday present there you go buckle you into

your little rocking chair and here's your giraffe Sophie and your winkle and let's clean the drool off your lip okay ready no don't squeeze Sophie Sophie doesn't have the right voice for this kind of song she's more a mezzo-soprano not what we're looking for here okay squeeze Sophie we'll work around her not like I haven't had to deal with my share of overenthusiastic background vocalists maybe I can cut her out of the master tape and that cough and that sneeze and don't cry pal nothing to cry about I'm sure Sophie's a good vocalist or maybe you're just not interested in writing a song but if I could afford a present for Mommy I'd get one though it wouldn't even be a present more like a debt and she'd see it in the checking account probably return it claim it's too extravagant just some earrings or a bracelet I don't know something to make her feel pretty but what's more important she'd say me looking pretty or some diapers for the boy yeah no brainer diapers but every once in a while something nice maybe and for the life of me I can't imagine what we'd do if I didn't lift your vitamins and formula and those stupid plastic toys well not lift as much as use the sweet Korean girl who runs the self-check line at Stop & Shop claim confusion with the machine tell her I like her green eyes and her hemp necklace but forty bucks for formula organic formula 'cause it has to be organic or else what you might end up like okay let's sort of cradle you take off the guitar strap okay get this underneath your butt and put your arms up here on the side and rest your chin there in the curve how's that better feel better feel sleepy all right sleepy is good this is going to be sort of a sleepy song anyway now what was that chord progression G to no C to F to A minor right then G okay C C C C C fucking A buddy you almost fell out of the strap don't make that face I know that face all right okay look at me look at Daddy it's smiley-time right isn't it smiley-time do you even know what the hell smiley-time means it doesn't mean anything that's right that's right keep smiling for smiley-time because smiley-time is a world that only exists in my mind and you won't ever remember that you used to love smiley-time until you have a baby and then you'll probably call it something different some inane phrase that gets stuck in your head and you're walking around thinking about a world where people have smiley-time at some point during the day standing still wherever we are smiling at each other and not with some condescending coffee-house how-you-doing smile but a real genuine smile that can crush your heart the way it does when you see true happiness on a person's face like when they're on a roller coaster or sled-ding down a hill whatever it is that makes them forget about themselves for a few minutes maybe not a good idea to have you resting your head on the wood so back in the rocker okay now let's get to work take Mommy into the past 'cause that's what a good song does takes you back in time sets you down next to old friends and lovers well hopefully not her old lovers especially not that Australian dude the two of them out in the wild looking at kangaroos taking peyote can hear that stupid accent in my head picture Greg Norman with Mommy's face in his lap while he says 'oy 'oy 'oy but what're you going to do that's the risk you take with a good song a good song brings you back in time a great song brings you to a place you've never been and you feel good being there Jesus you little bugger you were so relaxed there during smiley-time you went ahead and dropped a load right as I was about to say how it has something to do with our past and present and future and how they can work so perfectly together if you never think about time at all if you erase the concept of time from your being and just be okay that's ripe here we go put the guitar down gently diaper wipes a bunch of wipes and all right it's up your back Jesus how long has it been since you took a dump your mother never keeps me in the loop on your dump cycle we need a dump calendar or an eraser board guess we'll have to get you in the tub I've gotten a lot of thinking done in the tub over the years of course a lot of that thinking got lost once I got out of the tub because I never remembered to bring a pen and pad into the bathroom with me so let's clean you up and get a pen and pad and run the water and start thinking of lyrics for Mommy's song all right listen to the sound of the water listen to everything around you that's music everything's music have to make sure it's not too hot too hot and you'll get that pumpkin head screaming like a cat caught on fire all right me first got you up Jesus I hate the tub I look like a washed-up seal what a body no wonder Mommy turns off the lights and my nuts cauterized forty-two years old don't want to risk another well not a mistake no you're not a mistake but well we weren't planning on doesn't matter you're here you're beautiful you ready for the tub ready for the water okay here we go legs first yeah feels good doesn't it now your back and your arms don't worry I got your head I won't let you go under we'll just float you around okay it's warm isn't it you're gonna love the ocean maybe you'll be a surfer or maybe you'll build sailboats or maybe you'll be one of those guys who fishes in the summer and smokes dope in the winter and never really minds what happens around him because he's generally satisfied with his life and doesn't expect too much and never gets his hopes up and hasn't a clue why everyone's always arguing about what's fair and what isn't come on pal not in the tub well at least it's clear means you're healthy and you're smiling because you think you got away with something well okay we should get out of the tub not much thinking done after all but it'll come to us I mean you can't stop yourself from thinking it's impossible even wrapping you up in the towel and the tag says MADE IN CHINA and where in China it's so damn big though you have to think some factory where they're pumping out towel after towel all day it's towels or it's clocks or it's Elvis Presley key chains whole factories producing Elvis crap and not one of those kids probably knows who Elvis is or was or how if he didn't stop in at that little recording studio in Memphis or if he didn't shake his hips on *The Ed Sullivan Show* or die on the toilet or have this myth about him still being alive and all these wackos visiting Graceland like it's some kind of church then none of the Chinese kids would even be working the Elvis factory and it might be the only factory in their town so without Elvis they might've lived a happier life working a farm or fishing doing something outdoors where the air is clean and no one's breathing down your neck about printing a thousand of those "Jailhouse Rock" T-shirts by noon your skin's soft too soft maybe hasn't had to take a blow yet except that time you tumbled out of your little rocker but you knew to keep rolling and finally pressed up against the TV stand what's this spot on your belly spider bite do we have spiders fuck I hope not does it hurt when I press no good that's good probably bitten a few days ago spiders crawling all over the house can't see 'em maybe they hide until night come out in packs crawl into our bed down our throats that's why Mommy's coughing at night coughing on spider legs and what if they're pregnant what if they're delivering baby spiders inside us oh god okay let's zap those spiders out of our minds okay zap no more spiders get the diaper on your Onesie your little sweats and how about one of these sweatshirts a little chilly in here right can't turn the heat up past sixty-four heat's expensive if we hugged each other all day we wouldn't need heat at all zip you up looks like you're ready to get back to work are you ready to get back to work good little smile stick your tongue out make that fart sound all right buddy ballad in C for your mother haven't written a song a real song since I don't know when tried to get the band back together but Tamrod runs some consulting firm and Fido works a farm in Montana and Caesar's been cleaning toilets at Logan guessing drugs brought him there or maybe he's off the drugs and that's why he's cleaning toilets maybe he'll be ready to join up again in a year you only really need two founding members who am I kidding you won't ever know your father the rock star you'll probably see me as some old know-nothing like I saw my father until I got older and got interested in what his life was like before he started wheezing and coughing all the time and we needed to hook him up to an oxygen tank 'cause all I knew of him was that he was a finish carpenter he'd talk about staircases and mantels and window trim whatever but later he told me how he dropped out of high school and flew to Madrid and from there trekked through western and eastern Europe and to Egypt and down to South Africa and over to Chile up through South America Panama Guatemala Mexico basically traveled the world except Asia said he wished he could get to Asia and I asked him why there were no photographs from his travels and he said because it's all in my mind it's for me not for anyone else and I came to respect my father more than I ever had before and then well he died died before he got a chance to see you or even know you were coming said how he wished he had a grandchild all the men in our family since the dawn of time failing like it's a birthright to dream big and touch greatness and then crash hard I'm not sure your grandfather ever even went to the places he claimed to visit maybe he was dreaming up a more adventurous past for himself maybe I should too who am I who was I who should I have been for you going to that dark place again try to stay away from the dark if we can so what was the point of right well you'll see videos of me when I had long hair and purple suits and you'll think where's that guy he was famous he was weird he was cool but things change buddy people change and you're my world now and maybe I dream of getting the band back dream of me and Caesar at the Paradise but I know that's not going to happen too many mistakes band's got a bad name I got a bad name put down the booze and coke put up all that dough in a vegetarian restaurant called ROOTS which your mother said was a terrible name and I went with it despite her thinking if it stuck with me then it'd stick with others but it wasn't the name no one was willing to pay fourteen ninety-five for a plate of raw vegetables and even after selling the house and most of my old guitars and becoming sort of not sort of but becoming an actual laughingstock on the local news during a where-are-they-now segment claiming to have a connection with the spiritual world which I don't but I thought it might drum up some interest in my music again and maybe kids'll look up your last name find out who your father was make fun of how I used to look the music I played but you take out the synthesizers and you have some pretty lovely anyway it won't matter shouldn't matter 'cause unlike their fathers and very much like my own father I went for it and I did it and no one can take that away from me just like they can't take it away from you and I know sometimes I talk down about your mother but she's been with me through it all rich and poor and she deserves some slack deserves a break and she's a good mother to you and good woman and she's still the only girl I know knows how to give a decent foot massage and maybe that sounds like it's not a lot but trust me it's hard to meet a woman you can love all your life and when you arrived it seemed to make us love each other even more and I guess that's the point why it's so hard to write a song I don't have any songs left maybe you were my last song and maybe all your mother wants is a deep kiss and a warm bath and to be here with us a family our own little world just beginning.

THE PLACE YOU ARE GOING TO

~~~~~

WALLACE PRAGER LEFT Wequaquet early Sunday morning and drove three days straight, making good time to Buffalo Gap and Rapid City before heading south toward Casper, Wyoming. He stopped at a one-pump gas station and bought a postcard of a cat dressed up like a cowboy straddling a dog. The cat had a rope lassoed out toward a band of mice. The postcard read: *Wyoming*. He drove out to a state park and walked a trail to a set of boulders rounded and fallen in the shape of a sitting bear and tucked himself in the shade of the bear's foot. He wrote to his daughter, Francesca:

> Thought you'd think this was funny. You and I share the same kind of humor. Always have. I miss you and love you and I hope you're doing well. Make sure you're reading your books and don't give your mother a hard time. Now I feel bad for the mice.
>
> Love, Dad

He drove the hard, dry country until night and stopped at a Super 8 in Laramie. He bought a half chicken and vegetables from a diner and ate while watching a movie he thought he might've seen but couldn't be sure. He slept well and in the morning delivered his postcard to a mailbox standing like some lone impenetrable stronghold in the wake of the apocalypse.

He stopped in front of a van with a sign that read BEST HAMBURGERS IN THE WORLD and sat on a stool and ordered the only thing on the menu. The cook had pasted photographs of famous boxers to the inside of the van, and they were signed with notes Wallace couldn't quite read.

"All these fighters ate here?" he asked.

"Every one of them," the cook said. "Every one of them a champion at some point in his career. Except for Tyson. Tyson never ate here. Foreman ate twelve burgers in a sitting."

"Ali?"

"He didn't eat, but he let me take a picture. That's the only one not hanging out here. It'll probably be worth a good cent when he's gone. Not that I like to think about that sort of thing. But you got to be rational, even with someone who changed the world. I mean, look how much money Jesus takes in a year."

Wallace ate his burger and ordered another. They weren't the best he'd ever had, but they were pretty damn good. He drank a big cup of water and set a ten-dollar bill on the counter and as he was leaving he looked at the photograph of Larry Holmes and the note below his signature:

Dead meat, Red meat.

MOTEL SIGNS morphed the sky into a dull electric blue beneath the darkness of night. He took a room and washed his face and wet his hair. His stomach was upset from the grease in the burgers, and he lay in bed thinking of his wife, Gail. They had pushed and borrowed and stolen, and now broke was broke, and Wallace was searching.

In the morning, he showered and watched television as he dressed. A dog was stuck in a tree. It was a puggle, a mix between a beagle and a pug. A woman was crying, and she couldn't say all she wanted to say in the allotted news segment.

HE DROVE through the Rocky Mountains. People snapped pictures and saved them into digital memory. Nothing was forgotten anymore. He didn't want to stop. He didn't want to remember.

He ate a midnight breakfast and, with his bill change, bought a postcard of a sun dog over the mountains. Underneath, the postcard read: *Come to Colorado.*

> I thought the photograph was amazing, but don't try walking to Colorado, because you'll hurt your feet on the rocks. If that's not enough of a warning, I told a falcon all about you and how pretty you are. I said, "If you see this girl, pick her up with your talons and bring her home." So, you see, it's unwise to come to Colorado. Maybe one day we'll drive through all these places together.
>
> Love, Dad

He parked his truck at a clearing and sprayed down with mosquito repellent and bunched up clothing for a pillow and lay in the truck bed. He worried for Francesca. He thought about the way she ran, with her arms swinging wildly.

★   ★   ★

AT THE cross into Nevada, he stopped at a gas station and bought another postcard. It wasn't long until Vegas, but he wanted to get the postcard in the mail.

This postcard had a glowing alien head on its cover, and in neon-green lettering the alien said, *"Where am I?"* and, below, *Nevada.*

> I saw this alien today. He was very nice. We had coffee and talked about his planet. It's called Narafulaco-hardeeplin. I think I spelled it right. Anyway, I told him about the city we built and he said he'd been looking for a place to settle down and asked if I could give him directions, but I said I'd only do that if he checked in on my daughter. So he's going to visit you and then tell me you were doing your homework and chores and then I guess I'll have a friend there in the city. Who knows? Keep an eye out for this guy and be good.
>
> Love, Dad

Francesca and Wallace had created a city on the edge of an undiscovered ocean.

"This is so new," he'd said. "All we know is that the people who live there will be very happy."

"I never said that."

"Do you think they will be?"

"Not yet."

"Why?"

"Because no one knows it exists, so there aren't any people."

"First things first, right?"

Together they worked on the city. They built houses along the ocean's edge, but not so high that the people who couldn't afford to live in them would have their views of the ocean blocked. They were whitewashed buildings and the sun shone on their fronts and at certain times of the day people were blinded by all that light and when they could see again were stunned by the city's beauty, as though they were seeing it all for the first time. There were cobbled streets and fountains where water arced from the mouths of sea creatures and men and women cooked on the street and the smell of burning wood chips filled the air. There were no roads leading in and no roads leading out. The people who lived there arrived by chance, and by chance more people arrived after being sent a letter from a place and person they did not know.

"Why else would we build the city if it isn't the place you are going to?" Francesca had said.

"What makes you think I'm leaving?"

"I heard you. You told Mom and she told me when you were away this morning. I asked her where you were going and she said you said you didn't know."

"And now I know?"

"Yes."

During his last nights, they'd bought him a house on a hill on the outskirts of the city, overlooking the shoreline and eye level with the horizon. At times the water would turn gold. He slept on a balcony and woke up with salt on his lips and he could see the people that populated his dreams diminishing in the sky.

Wallace had gone to his bedroom and lain down next to Gail. She put her arm around him and fell asleep that way. It was a soundless horror, a body next to his, a mind unable to know any of his thoughts, unable to articulate a single truth about his life. He waited until her breath was steady and even, then lifted her arm and placed it by her side and went into Francesca's room with a pillow and blanket and slept on the floor beside her bed.

He did this for three straight nights. Francesca never woke when he came into the room. He would watch her then in what little light there was through the window blinds—a portion of her face shadowed, an arm, a piece of her leg, or maybe it was a scrap of paper, the outline of the city. He knew he would have to put her together each time much the same way when he was gone, though she would grow and he would not know that person.

On the final morning, he'd said goodbye and Francesca shook his hand as if they had made a deal, agreed on a contract, and he told her to be good. She asked him to send her a postcard from all the places he went, and when the postcards stopped she would know he'd arrived in the city.

"I'll send you a postcard from there, too," he said.

"Impossible," she said. "No cameras allowed."

"No cameras?"

"I made the rule last night when I saw you sleeping. I thought, What if there were no pictures? Then we would have to dream everything we had ever seen and everything we wanted to see, and no one could tell the difference unless they saw it with their own eyes."

WALLACE STOPPED at a large supermarket and bought a baguette and a block of white cheese. He ordered a cup of coffee from a stand to the left of the registers and sat and ate and read the *Las Vegas Sun*. He could hear video-poker cards flipping on screens in a bank against the far wall. Some workers were eating tacos. They chewed slowly, looking out of the dirty windows. When he was finished, he spun a rack of postcards next to a magazine stand and plucked one out that had a photograph of the Sphinx in front of the Luxor hotel. He put it back in the metal holster and spun the rack again and left it spinning.

He drove the long avenues that crossed the city. The lights changed from pink to yellow to blue, and he wished for twilight and solace and no pain.

He headed south toward Arizona. He passed a graveyard full of flowers and thought of the dead building cities from the roots of the earth. Maybe that was why everything was dying up above.

He drove until the desert spread out like a beach, its shore on the horizon, the sky an ocean. He tried to hold the image in his mind so that he could describe it to Francesca as the city they had built.

He had never been to this part of the world.

MUTATIS MUTANDIS

THE REASON WHY I went on *The Dr. Jack Show* in the first place? I wanted happiness. I thought maybe happiness had something to do with how I felt on the inside and how I felt on the inside had something to do with how I looked on the outside. I let myself go after Ron died, and then when Caroline left for school I pretty much gave up altogether. But I wasn't clueless; I could see my options like a cold sore on my lip: scrapbooking, movie night, yoga for beginners. I wanted a man to hold me and kiss me and screw my brains out. I wasn't going to become like these other women in town. So I took a shot. In my letter to the show, I said I'd put myself in their hands. Face, neck, breasts, stomach, butt, thighs, and calves: They're all yours.

A month later I'm sitting on a super-comfortable orange sofa in what they call "the quiet room," being instructed by Dr. Jack's bubbly blond producer, Melanie, on how to react to the crowd. She says they'll try to change my mind but reminds me that I've already signed a contract.

"Dr. Jack will also try to change your mind, which might confuse you at first, but don't worry, he doesn't really want you to change your mind. It's all part of the show. In six months you'll return a different woman, a stunning, magnificent beauty. Don't be afraid. Dr. Jack's hands are like the hands of Michelangelo."

All I can think is: What happened? I used to be rich. I drove a Mercedes and had a mink coat. My ring was heavy on my finger. We lived up in the Applewood Estates in a community of successful people whose children all played an instrument of some sort and put on concerts in the central gazebo on Sunday afternoons in the spring.

Melanie explains that Dr. Jack probably won't get into the children and the gazebo and all that, but he'll certainly bring up my husband's foolish death and my subsequent financial instability, because, naturally, a crowd would riot if a rich woman were being provided with free cosmetic surgery.

"You may want to consider crying, if possible," she says. "Think of something horrific. Think of a little girl with burn scars on her face or a puppy hit by a car lying in the street twitching. Those are just a couple of ideas. If you need more, we'll pipe them in through your earpiece; just blink three times real hard. Believe me when I tell you, crying is the only way to get the audience off your back. It's especially helpful in grabbing the attention of the audience at home, which we know to be comprised mainly of housewives and stoners. They stop what they're doing and wonder, Why are all these people crying? They tune in, turn up the volume, and then they tune in tomorrow."

Dr. Jack's show opens with the Fleetwood Mac song "Don't Stop." I'm introduced through a series of demeaning photographs: eating chocolate-covered strawberries while positioned sideways on a small chair; dancing at a bar, my hands up and belly exposed; caught sneaking a donut in the kitchen, Bavarian cream on the corner of my lips. There're not the ones I remember sending in. I try to imagine who was photographing me in such private moments.

Dr. Jack calls my name and Melanie gives me a little shove. "Don't stop," she says.

The crowd applauds. For what? Dr. Jack hugs me and holds my wrists; his hands are as soft as French milled soap. He leads me to a lime-green chair that's raised a half foot higher than your average chair, with a deep back, so that my stomach involuntarily folds to fit my posture. I lean forward and pinch my knees together. Wardrobe put me in a tight floral shift dress. They want me to spill out in front of the cameras. I spill.

I told myself I wouldn't cry, but, just after the weigh-in, here I am, crying. No need to think of anything horrific; the numbers on the board above the scale are terrifying enough. They brought out a silver square that looked like it was made to weigh cattle and, instinctively, I asked to take off my shoes. Dr. Jack said it's a myth that shoes add a significant amount of weight. My eyes were wet as the technicians slowed the numbers to create tension. They finally stopped at 208. The audience gasped.

There're definitely a few women out there who weigh more than I do but, at this point, I'm too deprived of energy to care. I feel like I'm standing in a swamp, sweating, unable to move through the muck.

Dr. Jack takes my hand and guides me back to the couch. Here is a photograph of what I looked like at eighteen. Prom night and I'm wearing a blue scalloped dress. My hair is swept over my upper arm. You can see the slim bones of my neck. My arms are tanned and toned. I'm smiling shyly, though I remember thinking then that I was too good for that school, for that prom, for those cameras. My date is Calvin Baker, the star quarterback for the Wequaquet Red Raiders. Besides some gray hairs, he looks exactly the same today. You broke my heart, he told me a few years back. But I'm glad you did. He was nice enough not to say why.

"Wouldn't you like to look like that again?" Dr. Jack asks me.

I nod, unable to speak as I stare at the girl I was.

"Wasn't she beautiful?" Dr. Jack asks the crowd.

Sounds that all suggest YES!

I can feel the spotlight on me now, the hard light picking up every imperfection. When I was twenty years old and a sophomore at the University of Arizona, I got a tattoo of a Yaqui Indian on the back of my shoulder. He's supposed to be performing a deer dance in which his arms are raised and one leg is in the air. Now he looks more like a crouching Sasquatch.

Dr. Jack is concerned with my flabby neck, my descended breasts, my popover belly, and my crimped thighs. He points to each part with a thin silver wand.

"BLAST AWAY!" he shouts. And the crowd joins him, "BLAST AWAY! BLAST AWAY! BLAST AWAY!"

Then it's a commercial break and the stage lights darken. Dr. Jack has makeup touch up his cheeks and fluff his hair. I look back at the photograph of Calvin and me, run through the life I might have had, the grieving mother of a boy blown away, how horrible, God, I sometimes wish I were her.

Lights up.

"We're back with Nancy Dwyer, who before the break weighed in at a staggering two hundred and eight pounds. Nancy's made the choice to change her life, and what a smart choice you've made, dear."

How could I turn back?

"I couldn't help but notice that over the break you were looking at your former self," Dr. Jack says. "You were her, weren't you? She is you, isn't she? You can be her again, but older, smarter, sexier. No more shyness; only confidence. Head up, body erect, stopping traffic on the street, causing an accident or two." The audience laughs. "Well, hopefully not. We don't want anyone to get hurt.

"And to prove to you, to the audience, to all the people at home, my skill with a knife, here are some before-and-after photos of other women I've worked on. This is Tricia with her crooked nose. This is Bonnie with her hopelessly flat chest. This is Sandra's—how do I put it nicely?—plump tush."

SUCCESS flashes across the screen—the audience is urged to shout the word along with Dr. Jack, throwing their hands in the air like a bunch of Baptists.

"SUCCESS in shaving down Tricia's crooked nose to a charming button; SUCCESS in building Bonnie two perfectly shaped breasts; SUCCESS in getting Sandra back into her favorite jeans by removing fifty pounds of unnecessary fat from her rear end."

Surprise! Here they are now. Who knows what these women are like? They could very well be psychotics. Yet the audience cheers. And who doesn't want to be cheered for? They wave to the crowd. They hug Dr. Jack and gather around me on the couch, legs crossed, high heels glittering. Their faces are caked with makeup. Sandra puts a hand on my knee. She seems to be itching it with her long nail, a nervous tic, I gather, a compulsion that hasn't healed with her receded waistline.

How have their lives changed? Tricia is married to a very successful lawyer in Manhattan. Bonnie owns a chain of lingerie stores in the Midwest that cater to big-breasted women. Sandra no longer feels uncomfortable flying or going to the

movies and recently got engaged to Butch, a muscled trash collector, who's sitting in the front row of the audience, pumping
his fist.

"All three of them were on the fence," Dr. Jack says. "Luckily, the mean dog of their past pushed them over."

Audience laughs.

Commercial. Tricia, Bonnie, and Sandra take out their cell
phones. Dr. Jack does some light stretching. Music plays, camera's on. Dr. Jack kisses each one of us on the cheek, then
high-fives everyone in the front row and runs past me and offstage. Show's over. The crowd is ushered out through a door
in the back of the theater. A woman shouts, "Go get 'em, girl!"
The lights dim. I struggle to breathe. It's a while before Melanie remembers I'm still out there. Like a little girl lost, I'm taken
down a hallway and guided toward a town car, which will bring
me back to my hotel.

"We'll call you in the morning," Melanie says. "Make sure
you don't eat for twenty-four hours. It's imperative."

I've already got well over a thousand friend requests on
Facebook, and most of them want to wish me good luck or tell
me how brave I am, while a few of the slimy ones, especially
Wendy Bishop from Seattle, who works as a pharmaceutical
technician, have posted on my wall a series of brutal-looking
photos of botched boob jobs and tummy tucks.

Later, I order a blueberry sundae and watch TV in my bra
and panties.

Last days of yum, yum, yum.

MY SURGEON isn't Dr. Jack. It's Dr. Stevens. Dr. Jack isn't
board certified—a bit of a shaky past.

"Someone that amped up doesn't have the patience for

cosmetic surgery," Dr. Stevens says. "Look at me. This is not a face you want to see on your television every day, is it?"

Without the mole on his chin or the pockmarked cheeks, Dr. Stevens could be quite handsome, and, so it's a mystery why he doesn't get work done himself. I don't pry.

First thing he does is draw lines on my body, a map of removal.

"Nothing is going to hurt until later," he says.

The anesthesiologist is young and pretty, with shimmering blue eyes and long, elegant fingers. She reminds me of my daughter, Caroline. I try to tell her about Caroline, but I'm already going away.

Strange dream of driving a convertible down Fifth Avenue in Manhattan, then up Lord & Taylor, the car leaping from building top to building top, until there are no building tops, and I sink underwater, picking up all kinds of sea creatures who speak to me in Spanish, and I can speak Spanish, too, and we discuss why it's best to live a spiritual life rather than a materialistic one. "Look at us," the bluefish says. "All we want is to live in the ocean and be happy." They swim out of the car and up toward the light shining on the ocean's surface. I leave the car and follow them. I'm awake in my new body. My new body won't let me move.

"How do I look?" I say.

"Relax, Ms. Dwyer," says a nurse. "If you move, you might just fall apart."

RESULT: FIFTY pounds of me sucked out and burned in an incinerator. Neck tightened, face lifted, brows pushed back, breasts pumped up, Yaqui Indian tattoo removed. Four months later I can pretty much walk upright.

What do I think?

Game changer.

Already I recognize men in cars at stoplights reluctant to go when the light turns green or how George Falachi dropped a gallon of milk on his son's foot when he saw me in the grocery store. Is it too much? Perhaps. But go big or go home, right? Do I care if Deborah Sanders snubs me at the dry cleaner's? Or that Gail Prager hasn't invited me to her father's birthday party? Not a chance. No time left to waste on what I can't control. I did this for a reason. Now it's like, where to go? The new me doesn't shop at MegaWorld anymore, not that their deals are anything to sneer at, it's just this body deserves high-ticket items, and depending on the salesperson—ring, no ring, bald, round, lesbo—it should be able to get me a pretty decent discount.

So I indulge, drive north to the Atrium in Braintree. What am I, a star? Well, sort of. Maybe it's just the breasts or the way my lips shine, or it's that people recognize me from *The Dr. Jack Show* or from the short money ad I did for Big Tim's Auto Emporium, but the lights are on me in every store. Maybe they don't know how I used to look. Now I'm having second thoughts about returning to the show, but roof over head wins out; plus, it was part of the contract—half now, half when you return, like some kind of drug run.

Outside at the Atrium fountain, while I'm eating my spring salad, a security guard comes up, and I'm thinking, Give him the "Can't you see I'm eating?" just for fun.

"Ma'am," he says. "I think a pigeon did some business on your shirt."

"Oh, God! My Marc Jacobs!"

I take a sanitary wipe from my purse and dab at the greenish-white stain. A group of women are snickering near the Chinese dumpling stand. I quick wrap my Versace scarf around my neck and get up to leave.

"Relax, ma'am," the security guard says. "Getting hit with doo-doo is good luck."

"Yeah? Are those poopers going to pay my dry cleaning?" I say.

"I've worked here almost seventeen years and never been pooped on once."

"Am I supposed to feel sorry for you?"

Then *splat,* right on my scarf.

"Twice!" the security guard says, and smacks himself upside the head. "Hot damn!"

TURNS OUT I've extended my credit as far as it can extend. The new me hasn't improved her financial status by much. Luckily, Caroline won the university writing contest for her story "Blacker Nights," which she wouldn't let me read but I guess has something to do with her and that basketball player, Rufus, and how he dumped her when they were playing exhibition games in Rome over spring break. Either way, she's a thousand bucks richer and kind enough to take us to the Asian spa. Hot stones, mud bath, facial: the works. The women can't stop looking. I go naked even when it's unnecessary, like through the lobby after the stones and before the bath.

"Mom," Caroline says. "Overboard, geez."

"Oh, psshh," I say.

One of those tiny Asians goes a little too rough on the gams and glutes during the deep-tissue massage. I see swelling in the mirror in the relaxation room. Nothing a little skin toner won't fix. As I'm applying, I notice Caroline's looking a little lumpy around the middle. I suggest a tummy tuck. She turns away from me. Her middle jiggles a bit.

"It's worth it," I say.

"To whom is it worth it?"

"To whom? Oh, God, you sound like Uncle Max."

"Is that a bad thing? Isn't he, like, an actual rocket scientist?"

"Yeah, and he spent half his life getting kicked in the groin."

"Can't say I see your point, Mom."

"Point is, sure, if you can break down algorithms when you're six years old you'll have a way out, but if you can't, then you'd better learn some way to take advantage of this world."

"See, that's exactly what I was talking about."

"You were talking about what?"

"Nothing."

Guess I said the wrong thing, but when I am feeling good, like after a few glasses of wine, I tend to talk over my head. I take it back, of course, because who else is there in my life besides Caroline?

On the way home, I remind her about the show next week.

"Can you believe it's been six months already?"

"You really do look a hundred times different, Mom."

"In a good way, right?"

"Sure."

"That wasn't a really convincing *sure*."

"Well, maybe; your waist is so small and, you know, the rest of you . . ."

She holds her hands out in front of her chest like she's carrying two big water containers.

"That's the point, dear. This is who I am."

"I get it," Caroline says.

But I'm not certain she does.

★   ★   ★

IT DOESN'T seem like women in L.A. take any shit. None of them get shit on. There're birds everywhere.

A black town car picks me up at my hotel, drives me to the back of the studio. Melanie greets me at the door and directs me to a private dressing room, where it's hair, makeup, and wardrobe. I'm wondering if this is how those other girls were treated. During the pre-screen interview, she hands me a piece of paper with five questions on the front, two possible answers.

"How would you describe yourself?" she asks. "Look into the camera when you answer."

Choices are: A) I'm gorgeous. B) I'm atrocious.

"Do people check you out on the street?"

A) People are always checking me out on the street. B) People run away from me.

"Two plus two equals four."

A) That's right. B) That's not right.

"If someone offered you a free vacation in the French Riviera, what would you say?"

A) You can't turn this down. B) I can't stand the French.

"What would you say to someone who wanted to physically abuse you?"

A) Don't mess with me. B) Go ahead, I deserve it.

After the question/answer, she tells me to flip the paper over.

"What's this?"

"Think of it as a play," she says. "You and Dr. Jack are the leads."

"But . . . huh, why would I harass a woman in row three?"

"Good question, and look, right there, where it says, Harass woman in Row Three, we've planted another actress who will be working alongside the two of you, in a supporting role, of course."

"But I don't want people to get mad at me."

"Yes! Yes! That's exactly what you want. What better way to show the world the new Nancy Dwyer than by drawing envy and jealousy and general hatred from those who cannot be you?"

"And this, in italics, *Wag your finger*—what's that supposed to mean?"

"You know, like—" Melanie puts a hand on her hip and stares out over my head, raises her index finger and wags it, and says, "Nancy don't take no lip. Or, you know, whatever. Improvise. Have fun. Listen, we've decided to go with a different format. It's not your fault. Dr. Jack doesn't know as much as people think, and it's hard trying to find people with debilitating illnesses or psychological problems who are both nonthreatening and willing to come on the show. My advice is to just go with it. Rock their socks off! You're on in ten."

A goldfish floats around on the monitor in the quiet room until the screen flickers and I hear "Don't Stop" and see Dr. Jack running up and down the aisles high-fiving the audience. He says, "We've got a special show for you today. Do you all remember the sweet-natured homely woman from Wequaquet, Massachusetts?" Yes, they claim to remember me. "Well, she's back, and you won't believe how much she's changed! Take a look."

Now it's a montage of quick edits and close-ups of me from earlier, with this spastic hip-hop music playing, and me saying, "I'm gorgeous," and "People are always checking me out on the street," and "You can't turn this down," and "Don't mess with me."

The audience is booing before I'm even out onstage, then

they're standing and pointing and pumping their index fingers down as if to suggest to Dr. Jack, with his despotic power, he feed me to a rabid beast.

Cue cards read:

WAVE TO AUDIENCE

STOP IN FRONT OF DR. JACK

TURN 90 DEGREES TO LEFT AND BACK

TURN 90 DEGREES TO RIGHT AND BACK

SIT DOWN

PRETEND AS IF SWATTING FLY AWAY FROM FACE

More boos, until Dr. Jack holds up his arms and, as booing dies down, brings his hands together and bows slightly.

Stunned. So much so that I can't hear Dr. Jack's first question, and not until Woman in Row 3 shouts, "Answer the man, bitch," do I finally snap out of it, feel full of anger at being called a bitch on television, want to show the world I'm not the bitch, she's the bitch, and she's got a big gap between her teeth and purple eyeliner, and the cue card reads:

WHAT CORNER DID YOU JUST STEP OFF OF, HO?

Then, well, when you see it—except for the curses, which I'm sure will be bleeped—you'll witness her running down the aisle and Dr. Jack's meager attempt to get in our way, and the sudden muscle deficiencies in the burly bodyguards as they lazily pick Woman in Row 3 up under the arms and let her kick wildly, catching my right eye with the toe of her heel, until the other bodyguard grabs her legs and turns them over and together they fold her up like a lawn chair and take her offstage.

Dr. Jack asks, "Tough being beautiful, isn't it?"

Given this recent experience, I can only say, "Yes. Yes, it is."

"Was it worth it?"

Silence. Blank cue card. Empty seat in row 3.

I think, Might as well go all the way.

"Damn right it was worth it."

MY MAILBOX is full of letters. Who writes letters anymore? Turns out the people who write letters are daytime-television watchers with a lot of anger inside.

"Hate mail is better than no mail," Melanie tells me over the phone.

"Well, can you stop sending it to my house? This one guy told me he was going to cut out my . . . you know . . . thing."

"How medieval," Melanie says. "According to our research, only point zero zero zero three percent of all threats are actually acted upon."

"That doesn't make me feel better."

On the table is a drawing in green crayon by a little girl named Amber, who lives in Wheeling, West Virginia. The two pictures are supposed to be me before and me after. The one on the left is a far-from-perfect circle, and the one on the right looks like a hot dog with eyes. Next to the circle she's written: *FAT BITCH*. And beside the hot dog: *SKINNY BITCH*.

"Listen," Melanie says. "We understand that our audience can be somewhat frightening, but if you were out of work and eating cheap caramel clusters in the middle of the day and your kids were screaming and the house looked like a demolition zone, wouldn't you find yourself overly invested in shows like ours? Try meditating. Dr. Jack, he squats against the wall in his dressing room with his hands covering his eyes for two hours before every show. Then he does one thousand sit-ups. Then he has one of his security guards punch him in the stomach until his hands hurt. His hate mail could fill a cathedral."

I thank Melanie for her advice, end the call, and trash the mail.

BUT FOR weeks the mail keeps coming. Everett stacks it in boxes outside the door and rings the bell. He's back in his postal van and waving through the window by the time I get outside. He's always been a quick, porky guy. Even in grade school, when he used to hand out the little blue notebooks to the class before each test.

I leave the boxes. Next day, Everett rings the bell and stays at the door.

"You have to take your mail, Nancy," he says.

"Who says I have to?"

"The United States Postal Service, that's who."

"Can you help me carry it in? I really don't have the strength."

Everett tries to carry too many boxes at once and the letters spill out on the floor. There's a card in one of the boxes from Donna Baker. It's a get-well-soon card. There's a child watering a dying plant on the front. Inside, the plant has grown tall and green, with lavender-colored flowers blooming from its leaves. She signed the card, *With Love.* No hard feelings, I guess. I'm the one who broke the news about Calvin and that chick he was seeing. Why none of us single women in town have gotten together, I don't know. Maybe I'll arrange a weekly wine-and-cheese night.

Everett puts the mail back into the boxes. His shirt has come untucked and there's sweat on his brow. I ask him if he'd like a drink.

"Got any beer?"

"Sure, I think there's a beer or two."

There's a six-pack, actually. I bought it for a guy I met online.

He said he liked this particular kind of beer and dried apricots and that he was looking to settle down because his life had been hectic and unforgiving. When the night came for us to meet up, he didn't show. I knew it meant he probably searched me on Google and saw a YouTube video of me on *The Dr. Jack Show*. But then, days later, the news had a story about a man—with the same name and photo as on his profile—spontaneously combusting like a bomb outside a CVS. He was married, had three little girls, and worked in a power plant.

"Here," I say to Everett, who cracks open the beer and slurps up the foam with his chubby lips.

"That's refreshing," he says. "So, I heard something about you being on TV."

"That's right," I say.

"I don't own a TV. But you look like you could be on TV. I mean, you look like a star."

Even though it's coming from Everett, I feel my face blush, the first pleasant feeling I've had in months. It almost makes me want to cry.

"Did I say something wrong?"

"No. It's just that . . . you're a good guy, Everett. People don't know it, but you are."

"I appreciate you saying so, Nancy."

He finishes his beer, stands, and tips his postal cap. I realize I'm nearly a half foot taller than him as we head to the front door. He turns back and blinks his eyes a few times.

"Remember when they used to call you Fancy Nancy because you wore those pearl clip-on earrings every day?"

I do remember. And I also remember how they used to call Everett *Tick* because he'd always be clinging to one group or another until someone shoved him away. I remember once at recess I pushed him and said, "Get away from us, Tick," and all the girls laughed and Everett smiled in this way where he was trying to keep from crying.

I lean down and put my hands on his bristly cheeks and give him a peck on the lips. I can feel his body freeze up, and then he nearly falls down the steps when I let go of his face.

"I'm sorry," I say.

"That's okay, Nancy," he says, stumbling backward. "I'll see you tomorrow, all right?"

WINTER COMES early. Snow covers the car and roof and lawn. The heat fogs up the windows. I put on Linda Ronstadt and play Treasure Hunt online. Later, I make myself a turkey sandwich. I consider my dresses and shoes. Last week I took all my old things to Goodwill, and just yesterday I saw a homeless woman outside Hal's, asking for change, in my plus-size silk chiffon cocktail dress. My scars are healed but still visible. Dr. Stevens prescribed me a cream, but it doesn't seem to be working. I put on a black evening gown, with white gloves and a fake diamond necklace. I bend forward, push my breasts together with my elbows, and blow a little kiss to myself in the mirror. My lips are too big. My face seems frightened by them. Oh, hell. I snap off the gloves and sit with my back turned to the mirror. I pick up a novel I bought one day when I was in the bookstore at the mall trying to get men to notice me. I'm not even sure what it's about. Lots of rave reviews on the back, though. The first line reads: *Maybe I was a dog in another life.* Inside, there's a photograph of a tired old woman with wavy gray hair, holding a pair of reading glasses up to her face. "You're a stupid cunt," I tell her. I change into my Juicy Couture shorts and bra top. After a good ten minutes of Pilates, I go out to the street and look down the block to see if anyone's coming.

*   *   *

CAROLINE CALLS me on my cell and asks how I'm doing. She hides her frustration well. Even at her age, she's aware that bright people can make mistakes. The smartest people in the world have committed the worst crimes in history, she says.

"I didn't commit a crime," I tell her.

"I know, Mom. I'm not saying you did."

"Good."

Beautiful is the pain on your face.

That's one of the lines I remember from a poem she wrote in the ninth grade. I must've done something right with her. Even when she was little I knew she was capable of sympathy. It's what makes her such a good person, why boys fall in love with her, and why she's able to write so well.

She says she's almost done with her novel, some interest from publishers. I ask her again what it's about, but she won't say.

"It's about me, isn't it?"

"No, Mom. For the hundredth time."

Then the doorbell rings. I wipe down the glass and see Everett standing to the side with the American flag stitched into his shirtsleeve.

A sense of excitement flows through me. I can feel it in my sewn-up belly.

"I got to go, honey," I tell Caroline. "Be good."

I open the door and Everett hands me another stack of letters, though it's a bit lighter than usual.

"I didn't expect you today."

"Neither snow nor rain nor heat nor gloom of night stays these couriers from the swift completion of their appointed rounds."

"Oh."

"It's the postal service's unofficial motto."

"I see. Well, come in. I'll make coffee."

He stamps his feet on the steps, unties his boots. The big toe on his right foot is sticking out of his sock.

"You have a hole," I say. "Take them off. Let me get you a fresh pair."

"You don't have to do that," he says.

"There's a box of Ron's underthings in the garage."

"No, I wouldn't—"

"Please, Everett. We've known each other how long? Now, have a seat and take off those wet, nasty things."

I put the coffee on. It's been a while since I had a man in the house. I'm noticing how plain everything looks, how I haven't thought about the rooms for months—cracks in the ceiling, dust on the shelves, vents clotted up with hair and dirt and balls of gray fluff.

"How do you take your coffee, hon?"

It comes naturally, calling Everett *hon*.

"Just cream," he says.

I nearly drop the mugs when I see Everett's feet up on the ottoman. I pinch my eyes shut, then look again. He has only four toes on each foot.

"Freaky, isn't it?" he says, wiggling them.

Makes sense now how he managed to get out of P.E.

I put the mugs on the coffee table.

"They work just the same, only no rock climbing for me. Don't look so shocked. I thought, you know, considering."

"Sorry, I just need a moment to adjust. I've never seen anyone with four toes before."

"And I've never seen anyone with such an impressive figure."

"Please."

"I'm serious. You've got to be the most gorgeous woman in town."

"You don't mean it."

"Do I look like I'm in a position not to mean it?"

"Drink your coffee, you fool. I'll get you those socks."

In the garage is more than just a box of Ron's underthings. There's his desk and file cabinets and the stupid wooden bust of Sitting Bull from when he went on a spiritual retreat to South Dakota and came back wearing a poncho and holding the bust in the crook of his arm. He said he had a vision during the sweat-lodge ceremony. He said he saw faces on his hands and legs, and in the dirt, too. He said everything is made of faces. For the next week he ate with his hands and took baths in a big metal bucket in the backyard. I thought I had lost him until later that week, when he was back to day-trading, screaming at his monitor, slamming drawers. He said something like, "Sitting Bull never lost a thousand pork-belly futures in five minutes," and that was the end of his spiritual awakening. Then July 4, 2006, and, as always, he had to put on the biggest spectacle in the neighborhood, drove all the way to the New Hampshire border to load up on fireworks, and, who knows, maybe those visions came back to him and that's why he stood over the lit fuse so long. Either way, I've seen horrific things before, so Everett's toes are no big whoop. They're actually kind of cute.

"It's funny," Everett says, pulling up the socks. "I've never been invited into anyone's house before."

"I should've; I mean . . . I don't think I was ever a nice person."

"My whole adult life I've delivered mail, never missed a day of work."

"I probably wasn't happy. I could never keep a secret. Now

it's like I'm the secret people are keeping from me. I don't know how to get outside myself, you know? I don't know how to get free."

"Even during that hurricane we had a couple years back, I remember the wind was coming from all sides, sort of holding me in place like a giant hand, and I had on my rain slicker, and my hat went flying off my head, and people had their generators running, and not one of them asked if I felt like holing up inside for a while. I ended up sneaking into the Putters' shed, and then the roof got peeled right off like the lid of a tuna can. Finally I made it back to my truck, and the rain came down so hard I could see paint fleck up off the hood. Next day, post office gets a dozen calls about missing mail, and I get chewed out for trying to save my own life."

"My mother used to dress me up and put makeup on me when I was little. Sometimes she'd make me sing for my father and my older brothers. Other times I'd dance with her and she'd lead. She was teaching me how to be pretty and subservient and stupid. She was a stupid woman. She made my father proud, and my brothers are both successful and have pretty blond stay-at-home wives. She showed them how to break a woman down."

"Every day, just before I head out on my route, I check my own mail first. It's almost always junk mail. I even deliver it, like it's any other person's house."

"Oh, Everett."

He takes my hand in his and holds it there by his knee for a while. I rest my head on his leg. He pets my hair and hums.

He keeps the socks on in bed. He traces my scars with his bitten fingernails. He kisses my neck, belly, and toes. His body hair is knotted. There's a pink birthmark on his side in the shape of California. He struggles to find me. I guide him with my hand. He's slow and gentle and loving.

He says, "Jesus," and "Oh, God," and "Yessah!"

He makes me feel full again.

And it's got to be the best feeling in the world.

ACTS OF LOVE

~~~~~

TARA WAS IN the kitchen slicing vegetables for a soup. I snuck up behind her and put my hands around her stomach. I pulled her into me. She pushed back. I tried to kiss her neck. She turned away.

"What is it? What's the problem?"

"I don't know. I'm trying. I've been trying."

"You have to try?"

"I don't like how it feels when you touch me. Please don't make me explain."

"Is it the baby?"

"Probably."

I went out on the back porch. That morning's snow glittered in the moonlight. I could hear Cal Baker's dogs barking to be let out. They went chasing after a squirrel, then stood around the tree like patient hunters until Cal whistled for them to come back inside. I waved to Cal and he waved back.

Everything was as it should be, except that Tara no longer loved me. Her not loving me made me feel boyishly afraid. Each room of our house seemed new and frightening. The same for the street we lived on, the town, and the office where I worked. I didn't know how to perform simple tasks. I panicked in the break room, grabbed at my chest, stumbled, and fell over the table of donuts. I was rushed to the hospital. The doctor said my heart was fine. He asked if I was under any acute stresses. He wrote me a prescription for alprazolam and referred me to a psychiatrist. The psychiatrist wrote me two more prescriptions. The pills made me feel heavy, and I sank into bed. I slept for three days as though sick from the flu.

Finally, Tara asked me to leave. She said we'd find a way to work things out with Colin.

"You named him?"

"Do you like it?"

"I want to be a part of his life."

"First take care of yourself."

"Please don't."

Her face was motionless.

WE WERE two men alone, standing outside our doors at the Affordable Corporate Suites near the battleship in Fall River, smoking, shivering in the cold, abandoned dogs too old to pity.

We wore knit caps and loose-fitting jackets and sweatpants and running shoes. Occasionally we glanced at each other, shoulders hunched, faces blurred by the yellow light flickering inside the plastic globes fixed above our doors.

We should have never known each other—not like this. We were lucky. We were men. White, privileged men. We could afford to take things for granted. Our dreams were attainable. Other successful white men mussed our hair and gripped the muscle between our shoulders and neck and called us good boys. We were good. Even when we were bad.

DURING THE second week I was there, the other man's car wouldn't start. I was going for my morning walk as if I had someplace to go. He asked me if I had jumper cables. He was driving a maroon Pontiac Sunbird, something out of the late seventies, worn and wheezing when it ran. I had heard him leave early some mornings. The passenger-side door was scratched and dented. He had New Hampshire license plates (LIVE FREE OR DIE), and the upholstery hung from the car's ceiling. In the backseat was a dog leash, a couple of water-fattened Robert Ludlum paperbacks, crumpled fast-food bags, and empty Styrofoam cups.

He had to pry the hood open with a crowbar. I watched him. He was a big, heavyset guy, with a hint of handsomeness he'd carried with him from boyhood. He lowered the hood onto the standing crowbar and attached the cables to the battery.

"That should do it," he said.

"I'll give it some gas."

The battery sparked when he turned the key. After a couple of tries, the motor turned over.

He thanked me and said, "You're in the corner room, right? Do you have a good view?"

"Of what?"

"Right," he said, and took a cigarette from his pack.

I understood he might want to talk and so I joined him. But we didn't talk. We listened to the motor rumble like a handful of change spinning in a laundry dryer.

I was hungry and the snow had started coming down. I went back to my room and made eggs and toast and sat on the bed in front of the TV.

The car ran for a half hour, until I heard the door slam and the tires spin out when he turned out of the parking lot onto the main road into town.

THE WEATHER had gotten warmer, though at night it was still cold. You could hear the residents of the Affordable Corporate Suites banging the electric heaters in their rooms. But the sky was clear and I could see the tall glimmering stars out the lone window of my corner suite. I watched them with the same blind awe with which I watched the television.

I had trouble sleeping. I took a blue pill, a yellow pill, a green pill, each developed to numb me into a state of irrevocable emptiness, where my thoughts and dreams and pain are flushed out into the space beyond space.

Sometimes I closed my eyes at four and woke up at seven. This happened both in the morning and evening. I tried masturbating. It was boring, or hopeless. My attention drifted toward the window, the frosted rooftops, the pink light that bloomed out of the sky at sundown and sunset.

TWO IN the morning, yesterday, or the day before yesterday, Pontiac Sunbird man was outside his door, reading the newspaper under his yellow light, his hands shaking, not from cold but from something else, nervousness maybe, or too much coffee. The skin around his eyes was red and puffed. He looked like a large child who, after threatening his parents for so many weeks that he was going to run away, had finally done so but now had gone too far and was looking for a way back home.

Maybe he doesn't remember me, I thought. People come and go from this place every day. We are interchangeable. To recognize each other is to recognize our own helplessness.

But enough, we are breathing, so let me tell you what happened the next day, today, when finally that Pontiac's engine wouldn't turn over and I got a knock on my door, my neighbor standing there in his coat, wearing a pair of jeans, washed and shaved, chewing a piece of gum.

He says, "This is such a morbid place. Let's get out of here for a while."

He holds out his hand, says his name, Doug. Doug Asplund, from Moultonborough, New Hampshire.

He's been doing survey work for the past two months. I don't know what that means, but it sounds just as boring as my job was, so I don't ask. This is the first day he's taken off work since he left New Hampshire. He's divorced and has two little girls who won't speak to him.

"Work keeps my mind from going dark," he says.

"That's natural," I say.

He looks at his broken-down Pontiac and says, "Let's grab a bite. I could use the company, and you probably could, too. I can hear you in the next room, through the bathroom wall. I don't know what person thought to build a place like this. I know your story, or parts of it, anyway."

Then he must have heard me sobbing the other night after I spoke with Colin on the phone. Though not really speaking with him but to him, saying, Hey, buddy, hey, little guy, what are you doing, you being good for Mama, are you having fun, do you miss your dada . . . and hearing his coo like a dove, his playful scream, his impatient sigh at not being able to reach through the phone and touch my eyes and nose and mouth. I couldn't take it. I had to hang up.

Doug heard how I had ended up here at the Affordable Corporate Suites. The guise that he was an indifferent guy smoking outside next door had been lifted. We could be friends. Or we could be enemies.

"Did you get your Applebee's coupon at the front desk?"

"What do you mean?"

"When you check in, they give you a twenty-five-dollar coupon for Applebee's. I thought we could head over there and have dinner."

I walk into the office but no one's at the desk. I wait. There were times before, when I needed more toilet paper, and eventually someone—a girl or the manager's sister—came out to meet me, having heard the buzzer when I entered. I don't know who the girl belongs to, the sister or the manager. She doesn't look like either. But all three of them seem generally content.

Doug is standing by the door, rubbing his hands.

"I could eat a horse," he says.

"No one's in there."

"That's fine. I'll cover the extra cost if necessary."

"I have money."

"No problem. I was just making a gesture."

"I am hungry, though."

"Good. Let's head out."

ONCE WHEN Tara and I passed by an Outback Steakhouse, she said that if you can't afford an extra ten bucks to support your local cuisine, then you shouldn't be eating out at all.

So we never went out. We didn't have any money.

But sometimes I'd sneak a quick bite at the Chili's down the street when they had specials or at the Cracker Barrel for their weekly fish fry. Something about the uniformity of those places is comforting. My waiter is always friendly and sincere; the food is hot and mediocre; drinks are strong and cheap.

At Chili's one night, I drank too many margaritas and fell asleep with the side of my face pressed against a plate of cold nachos. When I woke up, they didn't treat me like some skid-row drunk. We laughed. The bartender tossed me a washcloth. They had a picture of me on the wall the next time I went in, asleep on the nachos. I said it was fine if they wanted to leave it up, but if they wouldn't mind could they black out my face with a marker.

"My wife," I said. "Just in case."

But it wasn't my sneaking out for dinner or my coming home plastered or the moods of dreaminess I dropped into, a fishing bobber floating on the surface of what was real. I wanted to be a musician, an actor, a boat captain, a pilot, a seeker of precious metals. Time had run out. I was too old to start over. We had benefits, health and dental, and a 401(k). Tara instructed me to get on top when we made love. She said it was the best way to get her pregnant. I barely knew her. How could I know her? She was born with different parts. At my desk one morning, I flipped out and smashed my keyboard and flung my papers out into the hall. I drove the car up onto the lawn and spun the wheels until the sod and mud peppered the house. Tara screamed from the front step. I was blasting "Willie and the Hand Jive." Her face was freckled with dirt. I'd gotten to the bottom of the earth. There was nowhere else to go but away.

After two weeks inside Reflections, a rehab up in Duxbury, my insurance stopped paying, and I was back at my desk. There was nothing on it except the PC. I waited all day for a new password, but whoever gave out new passwords found a Band-Aid in his microwave chili cup and went to the hospital. The next day I got the password. The day after that it was like I never left. Months like days, then Tara standing in the kitchen; how beautiful she looked with Colin growing inside her, and how I wanted her more than ever. But by then it was over.

You can never go back to how it was. The time we went clamming on the shore and steamed them in the kitchen and then made love; or when we went up to Maine and stayed at the Fly by Night motel, where I sipped tequila from her belly button; or down in Florida, when she convinced the car-rental guy to upgrade us to a Corvette convertible; dressed like movie stars, we passed by the lines at the clubs into the VIP sections, living like there was no such thing as a past or a future, just living.

What could ever be better than that?

AT APPLEBEE'S, Doug and I take a table in the bar area. We look at menus. Turns out we can get two meals for twenty bucks and a free appetizer if we combine options from box 1 with options from box 2, but not box 3, unless we want to pay five bucks extra.

Doug wants a burger—"They butter the buns here," he says, "just like my mother used to when I was a kid"—and a Bud. I'm considering one of the healthy options from box 4, maybe the honey-glazed chicken breast sandwich. It couldn't hurt.

We order. We stare at the basketball players on the televisions over our opposite shoulders. The boys fly across the court like electric charges.

Neither of us has a stake in either team, and during halftime Doug sifts around in his coat pocket and pulls out a tiny cylindrical piece of red birchwood, one of those old birdcalls my grandpa used to have.

"This little thing is a lifesaver," he says, winding up the instrument.

We listen to it call out of context. Heads turn. The sound is as unpleasant as it is unwelcome in a place like Applebee's.

"My father gave me one of these when I was a kid," Doug says. "I could never attract a bird with it. I thought there was something wrong with me. Dad said to keep trying. Then one day, you know, when I was least expecting it, a rose-breasted grosbeak perched on my shoulder. I hadn't even twisted the caller. And that magnificent bird rested on my shoulder for no more than a few seconds, but I swear to you, I can still feel it there, the light grip of its feet, just the slightest pressure."

Can I tell you I'm on the verge of breaking down right here and now?

Because I am.

Even as he complains to the waitress that our Southwestern egg rolls are cold after he's eaten half the plate, or when he lets out an openmouthed belch after sucking down his first beer, or how he indiscriminately challenges the couple's conversation at the table beside us. Even now I want to just let it all go.

And you might think I'm crazy, because your Doug Asplund is so different from my Doug Asplund. But neither is really Doug Asplund, can never be Doug Asplund. You'd have to shrink down to the size of a gnat, crawl up inside his brain, and buzz around awhile to understand Doug Asplund.

What I'm saying, I'm saying, you would have to not be you.

By the end of the night, we are good and wet, stumbling back to the Affordable Corporate Suites like rovers in a new land. We shake hands, friends.

"Until tomorrow, good sir," Doug says.

"Until tomorrow," I say.

★ ★ ★

NEXT DAY I get a call from my cousin in Tucson. He heard I'd
fallen on hard times. He says he's been running a fairly successful contracting business and is more than willing to hire me as
an adviser. Basically, I'd make sure his books were in line. "I'm
no good with numbers," he says. He also says, "This is no charity gig."

But I know it is, and I couldn't care less.

For the first time in weeks, I welcome sleep.

Then there's a knock on my door. I open my eyes and stare
up at the water stain on the ceiling. I hear the knock again, get
up, and look through the peephole to see Doug standing there
with his big arms across his chest.

"My heater broke," he says. "Is yours working?"

"I was asleep."

"Feels like yours isn't working, either."

"I didn't notice."

He walks past me through the kitchen and sits on the couch,
rubbing his thighs.

"I used to be able to handle the cold. I used to be able to
handle a lot of things."

"I can make some coffee."

"Sure. Coffee would help."

I dump out the old grounds and start a new pot. I can feel
the cold now rising through the bottoms of my feet. While the
coffee brews, I wrap myself up in the fleece blanket they give
us when we check in. I can tell Doug wants to talk, but I'm too
tired to hear new stories. When the coffee is ready, I pour him
a cup and lie back in bed.

"This is good," he says. "Strong."

"I can't drink it any other way."

"I miss good coffee. Moultonborough has a little place that imports beans from around the world. I can still remember the smell of that place. I'd buy a pound and order a small espresso and sit outside when the weather was nice and watch the pigeons in the park across the way."

Maybe he's still talking, but I'm halfway to Arizona, visualizing heat as I shiver beneath the covers.

Then I feel the bed tilt and sink away from me. I can hear Doug's heavy breathing as he fixes himself onto his side. I don't move. Not even when he slings his arm across my body and slides up against me.

I begin to warm up. I close my eyes and slide into sleep.

Arizona is here.

So is Tara, and our past and future, the beasts of mind's creation, audacious acrobats flying from star to star. And Doug Asplund. Big, fat, handsome Doug Asplund, sitting alone on a bench at the edge of the universe, twisting his red birchwood birdcall, letting it unwind and twitter, until that rose-breasted grosbeak finally returns.

INCOMING MAIL

~~~~~

April 15

Hi, honey!

I probably shouldn't call you that anymore, especially if one of your bunkmates gets ahold of your letters. Do you have bunkmates? I know you said you sleep in trailers, so I guess they don't stack the beds in trailers, but maybe you still refer to each other as bunkmates, like in camp. You never did like camp, did you? I still have your letters from back then. I remember you saying the counselors picked favorites and that you were a better athlete than the other boys. You said no one liked you. Daddy and I told you to stick with it. We didn't want to get involved. Maybe if we were more a part of what was going on there, they wouldn't have made such a big stink about the fire. Anyway, Daddy refers to you as Private Baker when our friends ask about you.

How is he? Better! No more panic attacks. At least, I don't think so. We still can't go to the Steak and Sirloin for a while, because of his whoopsy, but I think that's more about them than it is about him. I'm sure there've been plenty of "accidents" in there considering how heavy the food is. He's taking medicine. He spends a lot of time in the basement, listening to old records.

Outside of that, there's nothing much to report. It's very warm here, so I can only imagine how warm it must be over there. I hope you're drinking lots of water and that they give you sunscreen. I'd send you some, but I think the air pressure causes the tube to explode. I'll have Daddy pick up those magazines for you, even though you know I don't like that kind of stuff. I probably shouldn't be writing this, but you're old enough now, and I think it's normal. When Daddy used to travel, he'd call me and ask me to talk dirty to him, and that was how he got over being lonely. So the magazines are fine and I bet they'll make you a hit with your bunkmates.

Which reminds me. I saw Caroline Dwyer last week on her spring break. I know you've always had a crush on her, and, MY DOG, she looks amazing. She's the captain of the women's lacrosse team at Cornell and, obviously, a brilliant student. I'm sure Kiki has potential, but maybe not the same potential as Caroline? Anyway, just throwing that out there. You know me, just throwing things out there, hoping they might stick. Remember when you were little and you'd try to catch my words with your little hands and put them in your mouth and swallow them, and then you'd burp and repeat the words back to me in a burpy voice? Daddy didn't like that, but I thought it was so cute I couldn't tell you to stop. I wonder if you remember being that young at all. I hope so. You used to make Aunt Becky and me laugh so hard we'd nearly pee our pants. That was the best time I ever had in my life.

Not that there aren't good times ahead for all of us.

Tough to imagine good times, though, especially when I go into Starbucks and right there next to the half-and-half I see the front page of *The New York Times* and there's always some photo of some Muslim's bloody or charred corpse and U.S. soldiers standing off in the distance. They never show the soldiers doing good things, like you say you do. Bunch of liberal know-nothings. It's like they're saying it's your fault because you're there. Well, weren't there bloody corpses before? See, you're right. I get worked up about it, and then I think, Look at all of us standing in line for our $4 mocha lattes and $3 lemon pound cakes (my little treat), and everyone looks bleary-eyed and, well, stoned, and I want to scream, WAKE UP! WAKE UP, PEOPLE! because they should really appreciate what you're doing more. That's what I think. I think they don't appreciate you like I do. This whole thing has really made me love you more, which I didn't even think was possible, didn't even think there was space in my heart to love you more than I did when you were born and when you lost your first tooth and when you broke your leg that time trying to jump the backyard fence and you squeezed my hand and didn't even shed a tear or yell or anything while we waited for the ambulance and the bone was sticking out of your leg and you looked right at it and said, "Cool." I knew you were a big, strong boy, but I didn't know you were that strong. Daddy says I shouldn't write you as much as I do, but I have so much time on my hands, and it seems like whenever I stop and think I get very anxious. This is about the only thing that relaxes me. I hope you don't mind.

Love, Mom

May 3

Dear Justin,

I've never known you to be so critical before. Sure, I've put on weight, and I guess I'm not the prettiest woman in the world, but at least I've got BRAINS. The last thing I want to do is have an argument six thousand miles apart from each other, especially in a letter . . . and, yes, I know I can e-mail you, but what's the fun in that? You just click a button and see words on a screen. There's something to be said about an old-fashioned letter with the person's handwriting on it so you know it's from them and you know they took the time and effort to make it readable for you. How do you know that if I send you an e-mail it isn't some Joe Schmo pretending to be me? Then he could make me say whatever he wanted and you'd think I was a crazy person.

Well, I guess you think I'm crazy, anyway.

All I was suggesting about Kiki was that maybe she isn't the right one for you. I think you have so much to offer a young woman, and to see you two together last time you were home, it just didn't make much sense. I mean, what she was wearing, it was like, "Hey, everybody, look at me!" and they were only really looking at her because you were with her. If she'd been on the street like that, they probably would've thought she was some kind of carnival sideshow act or one of those street women. I guess that's what girls from Falmouth are like. Trust me, Aunt Becky didn't look too good when I last saw her, and you know she's had her struggles with addiction. So let's call it even. You probably have so much going on that you don't even remember what you wrote in your letter. I'm not trying to criticize you. You're wonderful. Do I wish you'd come back and go to college and meet a young woman who didn't look so strung out? Of course. I'm going to be honest. That's what people appreciate most. That's what Daddy and I taught you. But it doesn't mean I don't respect your choices and YOUR honesty. Gosh, maybe I'm not even making sense. Maybe that's a good thing. Maybe I NEED to stop making sense. Daddy and I used to listen to that Talking Heads album when you were little. Daddy could dance! Did you know that? Can you imagine? Anyway, that was what the album was called: *Stop Making Sense*. Which I guess meant that you had to be fine with the world going crazy, and we were all a little crazy back then, but back then we were INSIDE being crazy. Now it's like I'm OUT-SIDE, watching other people being crazy.

If you enjoy Kiki's company and she makes you feel good and says nice things to you, then I won't say another word about it, except, sorry, but Caroline Dwyer is not a stuck-up B. She's about the smartest, most forthright young woman I've ever met. She visited her mother after we had lunch and asked about you and how you were doing. Of course, I didn't tell her what you said, but the fact that she asked, and, according to Nancy, has asked multiple times when you're coming home, makes me think she's worth pursuing, if you want. Did you know she's writing a book? She's only nineteen years old and already she's going to be a published author and I'll be able to buy her novel at the bookstore! I'll admit I don't really know what she has to write about. I mean, she doesn't strike me as someone with a troubled life, but maybe she's writing about vampires or zombies or werewolves. I don't know why people are so obsessed with the living dead. Maybe they need diversions. Fantasies aren't all bad, but to me it seems like people actually believe they can live in a fantasy if they avoid reality long enough. When I was a girl, we used to watch the news every night. Now it's almost like some people just think it's a movie or something, or they'd rather watch a bunch of cartoons farting around.

WrestleMania was on last night. Your father mentioned it in passing. He didn't order it—he doesn't really watch TV anymore. I think it makes him anxious. We were watching *House* the other night and all of a sudden he grabbed his chest and went into the kitchen and put his hands on his head and walked around in circles, breathing through his nose. I thought it was just *House,* but then we tried to watch *Law & Order: SVU,* and he went out in the backyard and lay down on his stomach on the grass with his arms stretched out. He actually fell asleep out there. When he came in the next morning, the side of his face had all these blades of grass stuck to it.

I remember you guys playacting wrestling moves in the living room and once when you pinned him down and he cried uncle and how that was the last time you two fooled around like that. You were too strong for him. I think that got him sad. He keeps saying how old he is, but I don't really notice him getting older. He still looks like he did when we first met— handsome, handsome, handsome.

Love, Mom

P.S. I started taking hot-yoga classes. Not hot in the way you guys say a girl is hot but in the literal way, because the instructor turns the heat up to 104 degrees so that we're sweating our beans off in there. I've lost five pounds already! Don't think I don't listen to you.

May 26

Hi, honey.

I've decided that I can't let my mind focus on the ugly. Like I told you, if you focus on the ugly, you never see the beautiful. Didn't I tell you that? I meant to, anyway. I need to practice what I preach, because lately it's all been negative. Hot yoga helps me sleep better, but in the morning I can't stop my mind from racing. You probably can't tell me, but I wonder if it ever comes up about where bin Laden is? They say this Obama is a Muslim. I hope not. I wonder what you think. Not just about the upcoming election, which, actually, Obama is claiming he'll get the troops home sooner, or at least have a deadline of some sort, but about what you really think on a day-to-day basis. What thoughts go through your mind? Do you see Daddy and me? Do you see your house and the neighborhood and your school and the places we used to go to when you were a kid? I guess if I'm being honest about all this, then it wouldn't surprise me that sometimes you have dark thoughts like I do, that sometimes you think what it would be like to wake up and know you're dead or that everyone else is dead and you're the only one left and how are you going to survive? Or maybe you try not to think at all, which is probably the best thing you can do, because if you think about the past or future too much then you're not focused on what's in front of you in the present moment. That's what I think of most of all. I think about what's in front of you, what you're seeing.

I was reading in *Time* about this soldier's wife who just found out she was going to have twins, when her husband was killed by a roadside bomb. I wonder if you knew him. He wasn't in your platoon, but maybe you crossed paths. His name was Roger something. Anyway, she found out the good news and the bad news on the same day. That's what made it a newsworthy story. Soldiers are dying every day, and they group the numbers together and say them on television or just show them with some sad music playing (then it's *Get Verizon* or *Buy a Toyota* or *Eat at Applebee's*), but they never do a whole thing about it, and even this wasn't really a whole thing about this Roger but about his wife and how, intuitively, she knew something bad was going to happen after she found out about her babies. If you ask me, that's just pessimistic thinking, waiting for the other shoe to drop. But I felt sorry for her, I truly did, and her babies, too, and how I'll never even know what happened to them unless *Time* decides to do a follow-up in twenty years, if there's even a *Time* magazine or any magazine for that matter in twenty years. Either way, I canceled my subscription.

Daddy says hi, by the way. He means to write, but when he starts he just ends up staring at the page and then crumples it up. He is doing better, though, I think. He's gone bowling with his buddies a couple times this month. He gave me a big kiss on the lips the other night (not that that interests you). It felt good. I can't remember the last time he kissed me like that.

Guess what else? I've started singing again. Granted, it's just karaoke, but trust me, honey, they take it pretty seriously. I have to drive all the way to Wareham to this bar called Tenderhearts, and it's mainly just older women like your mother, but there are some super-polished performers there. At first, I could barely get through a song I was so nervous. But all the women are really supportive and they urged me to just let go. Last night I got a standing ovation. I sang Melissa Etheridge's "I'm the Only One." You know the song I used to sing in the kitchen? You don't like that type of music. I never understood why you listen to rap music. I just don't get what they're trying to say. Money, cars, girls. It's like they're making you think you're supposed to care about these things even when you can't get them. Not that you can't get money and cars and girls if you want, just not as much as they seem to have, which is funny, because if you realized that, then you probably wouldn't want to listen to them, but because you listen to them, then they can get those things.

I don't know. I guess when I was your age I thought the same thing about my parents, how they didn't understand me and never would.

There's a big annual competition at Tenderhearts this weekend, and I think I'm going to sing a Patsy Cline song. I've been told that if you want to win, you have to sing something that's not too fast and not too easy, because the judges are all past winners or local musicians and they have very refined tastes. I've been practicing a few songs in the shower so that Daddy doesn't get suspicious and just thinks I'm singing to sing. Our wedding song was "You Belong to Me." Did you know that? You probably didn't. Anyway, wish me luck. The prize is a week's vacation to a resort in Mazatlan, Mexico. I think if I win, that'll be a real treat for Daddy. He needs a vacation.

Enclosed is a picture of him asleep on the sofa. I thought it was funny because he looks just like Andy Capp.

Also enclosed is a comic strip of Andy Capp, in case you don't get the reference. A big box of goodies should be arriving soon. Make sure you share.

Love, Mom

June 19

Happy birthday, my little angel!

You only have to wait one more year until you can have a drink—ha-ha. I'm not THAT naïve. I still can't believe it. That picture of you and your bunkmates, oh, you all look so impressive. When did you get such big arms? Honestly, I shouldn't be surprised, it's just nature, but how you've grown! You used to be the size of one of your biceps. You barely made it, after all. You only weighed three pounds and five ounces, and they had you on a breathing tube and a PICC line, and Daddy and I were by your incubator every day, watching the monitors and waiting for those few moments when you'd wake up and look around with those dynamite black eyes, and how tough you were, not even crying when they had to take your blood or replace your tube. And now you're so big and strong and powerful, it's really a miracle.

Daddy wants me to remind you that you and Moe from the Three Stooges share the same birthday. I never liked it when he called you Little Moe, but I guess it was funny to him, especially when he'd pretend to knock your head with his high school ring and make that cluck sound and you'd laugh and try to poke him in the eyes. He says happy birthday, too.

I'm glad you all enjoyed my cowboy cookies! It's a special recipe, as you know, passed down from your grandmother. I'll tell you the secret ingredient, because, really, who cares if it's a secret? It's just a cookie. Brown sugar, that's it. Not much of a secret, right? Not that you guys are out there baking cookies or anything, but in case you want to impress a nice girl when you get back.

I'm sorry to hear about you and Kiki. Truly, I am. I know I

said some nasty things about her, but it still hurts me when something hurts you. Sometimes, at night, I feel this pang in my chest, and I think, Has something happened to Justin? It's such a terrible thing to have to go through, because there's no way to know. That's when I tend to overeat. Hot yoga was becoming a little too aggressive for me. I kept trying to get into these postures and my back was killing me and all the other women in class were bending this way and that, and I just thought, I'm never going to be able to do this. Needless to say, I've put back on some weight.

Oh, and this just in! Your mother won the karaoke contest at Tenderhearts. That's right—WON! I mean, only four or five people showed up and they had already bought the prize, so it wasn't any big deal, but it sure feels like a big deal. Daddy and I are going to Mazatlan at the end of the month! I'll make sure to send you pictures. He doesn't seem too thrilled, but I think once we get there he'll snap out of this little funk of his. Now I'm practicing my Spanish. *Me gusta.* That means *I like.* Hopefully I like everything. *Me gusta* everything. I'm a little worried about all the violence there, but the travel agent says there's no violence at the resorts. Of course, she's a Hispanic, so maybe she wants us to think that. I guess if you can risk your life, I can risk mine, right? I bought a new bathing suit. It's sort of a classic one-piece. I'm a bit chunky in the middle still, but maybe by the time we leave I can lose some of my muffin top and impress Daddy. We've been married almost twenty-two years. Can you believe it?! When I met him he was in a band called the Fatheads. They were so terrible that it became kind of an event to see them play. He really was a great guitar player, but the lead singer couldn't sing and the drummer couldn't drum and the bass player just thumped the same note over and over.

It was hilarious. Daddy used to play for you when you were a baby. Sometimes I would sing. He liked my voice. He said it sounded husky. I hate that word. *Husky.*

I miss that time in my life, when you were small and Daddy and I spent every day together. I miss a lot of things. Thinking about you makes me happy, though. I know you'll get over Kiki soon. I'm glad you're not mad at me. And don't forget, Daddy's birthday is next week. I remember he said you were the best gift he'd ever been given. You can't imagine how many times I've cried remembering him saying that.

Love, Mom

July 4

My not-so-little patriot,

I'm actually writing this letter two weeks before the 4th so that it'll be a kind of treat to hear from someone back home on this very special day. I wonder how you'll celebrate over there. Of course, ever since Nancy Dwyer's husband died in that unfortunate fireworks accident, we don't get to enjoy the holiday the same way as when I grew up. Sort of strange how people clap over something that blows up. I mean, isn't the point that we stop blowing things up?

Your father's doing better. The other night he told me he loved me. He hasn't told me that in a long time. He's been getting out of the house more, too. There's some color in his face. Hopefully he stays like this. It's hard being alone when you're not really alone.

Please write, dear. Maybe you have and the letters aren't getting to me. Who can trust the postal service nowadays? Everyone who works there looks like they're on dope.

Well, have to start packing for our big trip. Can you believe it? Your father and me in Mexico? Hope I don't get Montezuma's revenge. Guess that's not an image you want in your head. Think of the time we saw all those purple martins when Daddy took us on that Civil War trip way back when. I know you remember, because you wiped tears from my eyes with your little fingers.

Love, Mom

August 10

My sweet boy,

I haven't written because there've been some things happening back home that I'm not too proud to share with you and it's gotten me so down I've lost sight of my main priority, which is you. I'll thank you for the card you sent to Daddy, because he's not able. What's a Haji? Is that what they're teaching you over there, vocab? They should be teaching you how to protect yourself from those crazy Arabs. I mean, they're the ones trying to kill you.

Anyway, about Daddy—

Well, first things first, Mazatlan didn't go too well. I had rented a boat in advance (paid in advance, too), so that we could go scuba diving and see all the wild fish down there and maybe even a shark! That was my birthday present to Daddy. It was such a horrendous flight, so bumpy the oxygen masks came down. The stewardess said they weren't necessary, but because of the turbulence, they stayed hanging there in front of us, swinging back and forth like a constant reminder that any minute could be the last. We landed with a *thud* and the captain said something in Spanish and so I was like, go figure. Then we had to take a bus with about forty Asians, who kept shouting and snapping photos, as if the photos would come out through the bus windows. Daddy spent most of the plane ride and bus ride in the lavatory, doing God knows what. When we finally got to the resort, we were put in this room on the first floor right next to the laundry room so that all you could hear was this whirring sound day and night, because I guess they do laundry every hour of the day, which makes sense, seeing that they have almost four hundred rooms. I went to the front desk and asked if they could put us in a better room, but the place was booked solid for the whole week (some kind of Asian corporate getaway). The toilet wouldn't flush and the air conditioner was broken. I guess they only had one maintenance guy for the whole place, because he said he had to get a part for both things and getting a part meant driving into the city. But he didn't come back until nearly seven at night, and he stunk like alcohol and tried to fix the toilet but ended up breaking a different part and he'd forgotten whatever part he needed for the air conditioner and started banging the sides with his hands. Daddy finally got fed up and went out to the pool and fell asleep in a cabana (which they later charged us a hundred dollars for, because that's how much it costs to rent a cabana by the pool!). This very nice woman said she could put us up in the manager's office on cots if we wanted, because the maintenance man had to get this different part in the morning and the prospect of a working air conditioner that night was slim to none (*manly nun,* she said!). She assured us that everything would be in working order by noon, and, because I couldn't find your father, I followed her to the manager's office and took my shoes off and lay down on the cot. Well, I've never slept on a cot before and never knew I was such a restless sleeper, but something about the travel and the problem with the room and Daddy's strange behavior made it so I flipped over in the middle of the night and sprained my wrist. I thought for sure it was broken. Oh, you never want to spend a night in a Mexican hospital, honey, trust me. But that's what I did. That nice lady came with me—Luisa, I think her name was. And you know what? When I was crying from hurting my wrist, she sang to me, and she had the sweetest, softest voice, and I told her she should become a professional singer, and she said sometimes they let her perform in the restaurant but that she isn't pretty enough to be a professional. I thought that was kind of too bad and I could see she was upset about it, so I began singing, and all the way to the hospital we traded songs, and she sang in Spanish and I sang in English, and it was really beautiful. When we got to the hospital she started flirting with one of the doctors. There was a man with a gunshot in the arm sitting across from me, staring up at the television with his hand pressed against the wound. He kept making these hellish grunting noises. I got him a cup of water.

Next day I found Daddy spread out soaking wet in his pants and collared shirt on a chaise lounge chair near the outdoor bar. Some unruly children whose parents had rented the cabana for that day began swatting him with these swim noodles, and he literally got up and walked right into the pool. You can imagine the eyes on us as I took him to our room. At least the shower worked, but your father had forgotten about the toilet, so . . . DISASTER!!!

Finally, we get on the boat and he doesn't want to go under. I've never seen him so terrified. I mean, he's been on boats before. You and he used to go fishing, if you remember, and I didn't think the ocean would be that different, but he turned white as a cloud and kept shaking his head, and even after the so-called captain gave him a nip of tequila, he wouldn't do it. So, after taking some of those Mexican painkillers (really just

Tylenol!), it was me with the fishes (no sharks, thank God!), and what an amazing experience. What forces created such colors? There was a point where I actually felt like a fish. I wished Daddy was with me. By the time I came back up, he was drunk as a skunk and was talking like a pirate and then went to the bathroom off the side of the boat, which the captain considered the last straw. I felt obliged to tip him forty dollars I was so embarrassed.

Some trip, right?

I guess an Asian couple got lost or sick or who knows, because a room opened up on the fifth floor overlooking the water, and so for the next three nights we had a great view and a working toilet and a cool, comfortable room. But Daddy didn't seem to care. He drank and slept and didn't set foot on the sand once.

I'll tell you another secret. I snuck out one night and went down to the beach, where they were roasting a pig, and ended up smoking pot for the first time since I can't remember when. I was so high, MY LORD! I even danced with these young boys who had tribal tattoos on their arms and legs. They both kissed me on the cheek, and one slapped my rear end. I shouldn't be telling you all this, but what the heck, you're old enough to know some things about your mother.

Daddy's in such a state I don't know what to do. My feeling is that he never really dealt with his mother's death, your grandmother. You were too young to remember her, and just between you and me and a hole in the wall, I didn't really think much of the woman. She was abusive toward your father. Not physically (though he used to make offhanded comments about a paddle that hung in the pantry) but verbally, calling him stupid and a waste of space, those kinds of things. I think he was glad when she died. Maybe that's what he can't get over. The guilt.

When we got back home, he went down in the basement with a package of crackers and a block of cheese and didn't come up until two days later. It gets to me, us being unable to talk like we used to, and I can't really talk to you, because writing and reading letters isn't the same, and so it's like I'm living on these images of the past, but I'm not sure that what I'm remembering is what actually happened or if I'm re-creating what happened to get me through the day. I remember during my one year in college, I took this philosophy course taught by some young guy who everyone knew slept with his students, though that's besides the point, and I remember him saying that none of us are really real, as in, none of us are really what we are; only a trillionth of a trillionth of a part of what we are is what we think we are. It actually kept me up some nights. I'd look at myself in the mirror and wonder where the rest of me was.

When Daddy came upstairs, I asked him if the cheese was a birthday present for his stomach, and he sort of smiled. I ate most of the cake I made for him and gave the rest to Nancy Dwyer, though I'm pretty sure she's off sweets, or can't eat them, considering all the plastic surgery (story for another time!).

Oh, well, that's that. They tell us in the support group to be honest with you, and so I'm being honest. Really, though, I'd like to hear more about what's going on over there. Your letters are so short. Maybe it's just always the same, but that's hard to believe. Hard to believe there could be more going on in Wequaquet than all of the Middle East! I'm at a point where I think I can handle knowing the truth. So, let me hear it.

Love, Mom

September 17

Hi, honey.

Writing this while looking over the photographs you sent me, and WOW! That's a picture of a spider? Well, geez, I'm glad you killed it. Who would think you'd have to shoot a spider?! It's like something out of a science-fiction movie. I have to say, it's strange that the first time I hear from you in almost two months is when you send me this awful photo. But I'm glad I'm hearing from you. And, yes, we heard the phone ring that night, and I actually knew it was you. I could sense it. But the phone is next to your father, and he just picked it up and put it down on the receiver without even thinking. Then I smacked him on the head and he woke up and looked around and went back to sleep. Seriously, sometimes I feel like I'm living with another person altogether. Your father is gone almost every night, and when he gets back he smells like he's been washing with a different soap and I say, did you take a shower somewhere, and he says he went swimming. That's what he does now, I guess, he goes swimming (and after all that happened in Mexico!). It's some kind of group. They call themselves the Late Night Lake Effect. They go swimming at night when it's cold. It gives them a rush. Of course, it's not something I'd like to do because I can't stand the cold, and your father knows that and it's probably why he's picked the most obscure group to join in all of Wequaquet. Afterward, they go to the Y and then have coffee and talk about God knows what.

Luckily your aunt Becky is moving back to town. I know you two didn't get along after you claimed she threw you into the deep end of the community pool that summer, but she's supposedly clean and sober and doing great! I'm looking forward to seeing her. I think it'll help take the edge off.

Please call again soon. I'm sleeping on the other side of the bed now.

Love, Mom

September 30

Dear Justin,

So I guess no one is speaking to me now. Between you and your father, it's as if I don't exist. And Aunt Becky, oh, I'll be surprised if they ever let me into Tenderhearts again. Despite the name, it's not some honky-tonk, and you don't take your top off and get up on the bar no matter how many guys are hooting and hollering and waving dollar bills.

I might as well inform you that your father and I have decided to take a little "break" from each other. Actually, I decided. Whatever he told you (and I know you've been chatting, because the last time we spoke, he said that you were upset about how worried I was and that you needed to be focused on yourself, not on me, which makes sense, but even if I was in the Congo I'd still be thinking about you and Daddy), he probably didn't tell you all of it. I won't go into the dirty details, but you deserve to know. Let's just say your father has found a new person to spend his time with. I guess I could see it coming. He's been out every night with the Late Night Lake Effect and there are men and women in the group, and you know how it is when you have something in common with someone. According to the rumors, your father has been spotted getting very close with a woman at a Dunkin' Donuts in Falmouth. Go figure! So, what did I do? Well, I let it go for a while, until a few nights ago when the phone rang and I thought it might be you calling, and I reached over and picked it up and said, "Hello?" and

I could hear someone breathing on the other end and they hung up. Then I realized your father wasn't in bed. So I dialed *69 and a woman answered and said, "Hey, sexy pants," whatever the hell that means, and I said, "This is NOT sexy pants!" And she said, "How did you get this number?" And I said, "It was pretty simple, stupid." And she said, "I know all about YOU, missy." And I said, "Oh, then you know that if I ever find out who you are, I'll cut your nipples off." Can you believe that?! I literally have no idea where that came from, but I said it, and she hung up, and I sat there in bed with the phone in my shaking hand, and I could feel this violence flow through me, and I threw the phone through the window, which wasn't very smart because it's freezing out, in September!—so much for global warming—and so I had to get some extra blankets from the closet and that's where I saw your father's wet suit, hidden underneath the summer linens, and I knew he wasn't going out with the Late Night Lake Effect anymore; he was seeing this woman! And so what happened that night when she called was that he was on his way to her place (dressed in his SEXY PANTS, I assume) and stopped to help this guy who was standing in the middle of Isaac Road, waving his hands. I guess he was part of a carnival or something, because he was hauling the fattest man in the world in this trailer, but the trailer had come unhitched and he didn't have the strength to pick it up and the fat man was in the trailer crying and the whole thing was like an awakening for your father because, and this is him talking now, he could see how hiding this giant secret was eventually going to cause him to break down. What a freaking metaphor! He ended up dislocating his shoulder getting the trailer up on the hitch, and the carnival guy had to drive him to the hospital, so that's why this woman was looking for him. I didn't know anything about it until he came home around four the next morning with his arm in a sling and I was up, sitting at the kitchen table, having had so much coffee my temples were pounding, and you know what the first thing your mother did was? The first thing I did was console the man. I actually pretended like that woman never called and like I didn't see the wet suit in the closet, and even when he asked why it was so drafty in the house, I pretended like there wasn't a broken window in the bedroom, and I put my arms around him and he said, careful, and I held him, and he said he thought he might be too old to go swimming at night, and I said maybe that's true. Can you believe that? I accepted the lie before he even told it. And I know why. It's because I'm scared to be without him. I can't remember the last time I thought about what to do with a day that didn't include you or your father. Then I thought, Can I change? I mean, look at Justin, he's strong and brave and doing what I could never imagine doing, and now look at Daddy, he's fought through depression and having his son gone and was able to find a new woman at his age. I actually envied him. I thought: Why can't I go out there and do something different, too? So, you know what I did? I got in the car and drove to New York City. Just on a whim! I didn't even know how to get to Manhattan, and I pulled into a gas station and this nice (what do you call them? Hajis?), this nice Haji told me I was in the Bronx and gave me directions on how to get to Midtown and then I saw all the lights in Times Square and I nearly crashed because everything was so overwhelming. I asked someone who looked like he lived in Manhattan which was the fanciest hotel in the city, and he said it depended on what my idea of fancy was, and I said I was looking for a place with big crystal chandeliers, which to him, I guess, meant an old kind of fancy, and so he told me the Pierre, and I knew I'd heard of the Pierre or seen it in a movie, and so I just left the car parked there in Times Square and took a cab to the Pierre and asked the hotel clerk if they had any suites. I didn't even care about the price. They must've thought I was some kind of big deal, because all of a sudden there were two bellhops at my side, asking me if I needed help with my luggage, and I said I didn't have any luggage—I was planning on going shopping the next day—and they nodded and led me to my room and showed me how everything worked and even unwrapped a giant basket of fruit and cheese that was on the oak table in the dining area of the suite. Then you know what one of these men said to me? He said, "It gets lonely in a city this big," and gave me this look like he could help relieve me of this loneliness if I just gave him the okay, but that's not what I was looking for. I didn't want another man. I wanted to be alone, and I told him so and tipped him and the other bellhop and ordered them to have a dish of chocolate-covered strawberries brought up right away. Can you imagine? Your mother in a suite in New York City, ordering grown men to bring her chocolate-covered strawberries! I'll tell you I had the best sleep in my entire life in that bed, and when I woke up, I was looking right over Central Park, over the whole city, like some kind of queen, and all the people below were so small and they all looked the same, and it came to me that it didn't matter what any of us did, because, look at all these people, they don't know me and I don't know them, but we're all moving through the world doing whatever it is that we do and we don't really know what that is and we don't have time enough to find out and so better to do what you really want to do with the time you have. That's what I figured out in New York City. And when I got home, I told your father I knew what he was doing and I wasn't mad and I understood but that we couldn't live together anymore.

And now, for the first time in my life, I feel truly free. I don't have to worry anymore. I don't have to concern myself with other people. Their life is not my life.

I hope you don't think your mother's nuts. I don't think I am. Lately I feel like there's this voice that flows through me, something beyond the world, and it tells me to relax and be calm, everything's going to be all right. And for the first time in my life I believe that's true.

I know this might not make much sense, honey. But how can I possibly explain to you what it's like to be me?

Love you with all my heart and soul.

Mom

OKAY SEE YOU SOON
THANKS FOR COMING

~~~~~~

DAD PULLS UP in his Lincoln Navigator with his new girl-friend, Roxy. She has spiky black-and-blond hair and makeup to match her hair and a loose blouse, so loose that when she breaks her heel in the pothole in the driveway, one of her big fake boobs pops out. Makes me laugh so hard I can barely breathe. Kit gets the bag and I take big breaths into the bag, looking out the window as Dad helps Roxy up to the steps and rubs her toes.

"Feel better?" Kit asks.

"I swallowed a boog."

"I can't stand how sexy you are when you can't control yourself."

"Baby," I say.

I crumple up the bag and toss it behind the couch, meet Dad at the front door, and say, "Let me smell your hands."

"Let's not," he says.

"The baby," I say.

He lets me smell them.

"Yep, need to get you in the decontamination chamber."

"What's that?" Roxy says.

Dad gives her a look like, Didn't we talk about this on the ride up?

At least Roxy speaks English. Dad's last girlfriend was some Puerto Rican named Lupe, who was five years younger than me. Kit and I went down for Christmas, and his house was all done up with depressing scenes of Jesus dying on the cross, votive candles, dead flowers. Dad was watching basketball on TV and Kit gave me a look like, Possible bonding moment? And even though it smelled like Lupe was cooking a pot of trash, Kit went into the kitchen to help out. So I asked Dad what the score was, even though it was clear what the score was, because I could see it on the banner at the bottom of the screen.

Dad said, "You need glasses or something?"

Then he changed the channel to CNN, a special about heroes, and this hero being a guy who built an irrigation system in some dried-out village in India.

"That's impressive," I said.

And Dad said, "What's impressive is putting a roof over your family's head. That's a hero."

He was talking about himself, of course. He did put a roof over my head, for a while. But all these muddy Indians slurping up water and smiling and high-fiving the guy/hero and his team—

"How long have you and Lupe been together?"

"Since last month."

"Moved right in, huh?"

"It's like living with a maid. I might marry this one."

And I guess she was a good woman to have around. She sure was sexy, but, problem was, no one could understand what she was talking about. Unless of course you remembered to bring your Spanish phrase book. Lots of nodding during dinner. Lots of passing around whatever that dish with the bone sticking out of it was.

When we left, Lupe gave me a big kiss and said, *"Feliz Navidad!"*

Kit spent all night in the bathroom and came out the next morning with her head shaved, which was pretty cool actually.

Middle of January, Dad said he was cleaning out the stable again, meaning no more Lupe.

At the sink next to the stacked washer-dryer, Roxy seems confused about what she's supposed to be doing here.

In my mind I'm like, Hey, Roxy, haven't you ever seen an industrial-size tub of orange crystals and a horse brush?

Then she goes, "But, Poopy, my nails."

"She calls you Poopy?"

"It's just a nickname," Dad says.

"So you don't mind if I call you Poopy, too?"

"Don't get cute. Where are the towels?"

I grab some towels.

"You need to scrub your arms, hands, and fingers for exactly two minutes. Remember to get between your fingers. I'll start the timer once the water heats up."

I stand outside the door with the egg timer. I hear Roxy say she can't feel her hands, it's like she has no hands. Good. That means all the critters in her skin are dying. Somber joy at seeing the old man in an apron. Somber because V3's a preemie and his body is still slightly curved like an *S* and there's a bruise on top of his head from where he got stuck in Kit's uterus and because we don't know how he'll turn out developmentally; Dr. Duncan says it's out of our control, a wait-and-see. Dr. Duncan doesn't believe in the nurture theory. Of course, we'll still love him even if he isn't mentally all there, because, really, who is?

"Okay," Dad says.

I check their hands and fingers for any possible debris.

"We're clean. Where is it?"

"It?" I say.

"The baby. The boy, I mean. Where's my grandson?"

A big thump in my chest at hearing him say *grandson* for the first time.

I LIMIT Roxy's interaction to approximately twenty seconds. At sixteen seconds, Vincent Three gets squirmy and she says, "He's like a wet noodle," which, do you have any idea how offensive? I cradle him in my arms and carry him to Dad, who has been carefully avoiding V3 since we walked into the nursery, instead studying the framed paintings of anime stills, which Kit and I collect and trade, flipping open the baby book to the first pages of V3 with his head bloodied and wing split, covered in plastic wrap, purple and blue, scale reading two pounds, ten ounces. He claps the book shut.

Roxy is making faces at V3, and at last he's overwhelmed and his face goes pumpkin orange and he starts wailing like a red-tailed hawk.

Dad turns and looks at V3.

"Boy has some pipes on him, doesn't he?"

"You want to hold him?" I say.

"Maybe when he's calmed down," he says, and takes Roxy's hand.

I hold V3 under the arms. He likes hanging there. He stops screaming and stares at me like I'm a Martian.

"Goo," he says, with those wide black endless universes.

AFTER BABY-VIEWING is over, Dad asks if there's coffee and I say sure and we go into the kitchen and I put the coffee on.

Dad says, "You look good, Vincent."

Whoa, compliment! But pretty sure he's just saying it to say it, because I look exactly the same as I did at Christmas, when he told me I could stand to lose a few. All my life I've been chubby, but Kit loves me chubby. She lays her head on my belly and falls asleep. She says I'm like a big, soft pillow. What's more comfortable than a big, soft pillow? And so there's no reason not to be chubby if Kit loves me, because she's all I really care about, she and Vincent Three, and right now V3 loves everything and everybody, even Grandpa, Dad.

We watch the coffee percolate. Kit comes in and twirls her finger next to her head, her way of saying, Chick is whacked.

Roxy isn't far behind.

"I was just telling your son's wife about my book," Roxy says.

Dad looks at me like, Please don't.

"What about your book?" I ask.

"It's a children's story, but it's based on my life growing up, which wasn't all that pleasant. My father had a lot of people after him about money, and one night he tried to rob a check-cash place with a water pistol and the guy behind the counter shot him in the chest. My sister and I were orphaned. My mother had left before I could know what she looked like. I'm gonna call it *Toy Guns and Broken Hearts*."

"Pretty catchy title, don't you think?" Kit says, grinning.

"I'm writing it because I think there're a lot of kids who don't have nice homes and can relate, you know?"

"Don't kids read books to escape their crappy home life?" I say, and glance at my father.

"See, my thinking is that this idea of escape is what's making kids so crazy. If they had a little bit more reality in their lives, then they wouldn't be shooting up schools."

"Not too big a leap, Kermit," Kit says.

"What did she call me?"

I give Kit a look like, Maybe take it down a notch, because I know she's being smart and at this point Roxy is making me anxious and a little depressed.

"Almost time for dinner?" I ask Kit.

"Sure," she says. "I get it."

FIRST THING Dad and Roxy notice is no chairs, just cushions around the coffee table.

"We're going tribal," I tell Dad.

Kit loves curries. She's got a blog called *Curry Whore,* where she posts about this or that curry. I'm a dumpling guy myself. But I can go for just about anything. Tonight, though, we're having roasted lamb chunks and asparagus and a batch of injera Kit has made from scratch.

When I was a kid, I used to scoop the center out of my dinner roll and stuff as much food as I could inside. Then Dad would take my plate and dump it on the floor of the mudroom, where we kept our shoes and jackets and sports equipment. "Eat," he'd say. "Just like a pig." Now, tables turned. No utensils in this house. And what are you going to wipe your hands with? Your tongue, dummy!

"This is how the Ethiopians do it," I say.

"Not all Ethiopians," Roxy says.

Hmm. Sensing Roxy has some sort of secret involving a man of Ethiopian descent.

Looks like Dad's decided not to eat, and after one bite Roxy's thinking maybe this might do a number on her insides, but Kit and I eat like it's our last meal. We don't care about the grease or gas or especially the mess. Sometimes we have naked day and just do what we'd normally do but in the buff. We're natural sorts. We do what we want. That's why we love each other so much. She gets me and I get her. You can't love someone unless you get them. All of a sudden it just happens, and you're both like, all right, power on.

"Where did you two meet?" I ask.

"You want to tell him?" Roxy says.

"You go ahead," Dad says.

"Well, it all sort of started back when my ex-husband and I were looking for a house on the Outer Banks, and so someone recommended your father, and he was so charismatic, and . . ."

As Roxy drones on, I look at Kit and imagine her with seven heads and how much fun that'd be to get one talking about one thing and another about another thing, and maybe the third one could sing and the fourth could give me kisses, and the fifth could start arguing with the first and second about how they don't know what they're talking about concerning the things they're talking about, and the sixth and seventh would keep watch for photographers who might have heard the rumors about a woman with seven heads.

Roxy says, "Are they even listening?"

I look at Kit on her phone, probably playing Zombie Tsunami, which, go ahead, try to beat my score, babe.

"Honey," Dad says. "That's just their way."

"Yeah," Kit says, looking up from her phone. "It's our way."

"We appreciate you having us over, son, but maybe it's time we get going."

"Wait," I say.

On the mantel are an assortment of misshapen bowls, ashtrays, and mugs from when Kit's stepdad took pottery during his two years on unemployment. They basically stand for, Look, here's a guy who was really bad off and he still tried to do something worthwhile, even though he failed. So some significance attached.

I take down a bowl that's sort of oval shaped, with a kind of mossy-green color to it and the initials R.I.P. in red at the bottom, which, those are his initials—Richard Ivan Pearly—and, sure, why not have a little fun if, say, someone decides to fill the bowl with a bag of mini-donuts or M&M's or nacho cheese, then you'd be like, you know, this bowl is telling me something.

"For you," I say, and hand the bowl to Roxy.

Her eyes brighten.

THE RAIN turns to snow and starts sticking to the mulch and grass and pavement. Soon the cars are covered. Then some tree branches snap, and Kit and I run to the living room to make sure we message the rest of our team that a possible power outage could prevent us from taking Germany.

I hear Roxy in the dining room saying something like, "This entire generation sees the world through screens. It's ludicrous."

I say to Kit, "Someone's taking twenty-first-century philosophy at the Community U."

Kit snorts.

Team says they'll make camp, but how long they can make camp they're uncertain, plus all the artillery Kit and I have collected over the past few months and my skills as a first-class sniper, they'd hate to lose us, but if the Germans discover the camp—

"Fucking hypothetical, Jarvis!" Kit yells.

I love it when she gets mad. Her whole forehead wrinkles up, and these little bubbles of spit pop at the corners of her lips.

"You and Dave take some bong hits and eat some Doritos. We have company."

But Kit knows this isn't a viable excuse. Neither is the baby. At least with the baby I can put him in the Björn and keep playing. I wonder what it would be like if I put Dad in the Björn and carried him around the house.

"What's so funny?" Kit asks.

"I'll tell you later," I say. "You'd fart if I told you now."

Which is true, because that's what Kit does when something's crazy hysterical.

DAD AND Roxy are discussing dining options given the inclement weather. Dad grips the back of my neck, says, "You're doing good with that boy, you know."

I almost want to cry, that's how overwhelming it can get when Dad is kind.

Roxy sniffs her nails.

"I'd like to see that little guy one last time, but I don't want to have to use that stuff," she says.

"You're not really leaving so soon?" I say.

"Looks like a nasty storm coming, bud, and Roxy's starving."

"So?" Roxy says.

"I guess," I say, because maybe she's the best Dad can do.

Vincent Three is wrapped snugly, sleeping peacefully, his head like a large grape sticking out from his swaddling blanket.

"Oh, dear," Roxy says, grinning so hard I can picture her face breaking apart.

I hear one of the Xbox controllers crack against the wall in the other room. Clearly the camp didn't hold and our unit moved on without us. Kit's devoted to our fantastical cause, the same as she's devoted to me and to Vincent Three and our life together, our family.

"Shit-suck-fucker," she shouts from the other room.

V3 spits up on Roxy's blouse.

"Christ," she says. "Do you know how much?"

Dad takes V3 and cradles him while Roxy runs to the sink, her boobs bopping up and down.

I feel bad for Dad, bad and sad, the way he probably felt for me the time he took me to meet a girl at the Putt-Putt and she didn't show and I played all eighteen holes alone, and when I was at the eighteenth hole I saw Dad sitting in the car, waiting, and I knew he hadn't left, but I also knew he believed I should feel hurt—his reasoning being that he had been hurt before, has been hurt since, and unless you know that hurt, you can't know love.

When Roxy snaps her fingers, Dad hinges his neck away from Vincent Three, then hands me my boy. With a look of joy-lessness and sorrow, he takes hold of my shoulders and gives me a kiss on the forehead.

"Thanks for having us," he says.

"No problemo," I say.

And with that he nods, as if confirming something we both know but can't say.

FRIEDA, YEARS LATER

～～～

THIS MORNING LEONARD Putter's kids are poking their bellies, asking if something is wrong with their stomach hole.

"It burns," they say, scratching.

"You have to wash better," he tells them.

"You and Mommy didn't teach us that," they claim.

Surely we did, Leonard thinks. Surely we showed them how to wash and they watched us wash and watched us wash them.

But maybe they're right. Of all the things he can remember, Leonard can't remember teaching them how to clean their navels. Or brush their teeth. Or clip their nails. In fact, both Lucy and Teddy are nail-biters. Cindy's always smacking their hands away from their mouths.

"Go on and play," Cindy says. "Mommy and Daddy are talking."

She sips her coffee, looks at Leonard despairingly.

"Don't pity me," Leonard says.

Last night he'd begun fondling her. Then she said, "To the left," in a harsh, sexless voice. He rubbed her clitoris as though it were a spot on the counter that wouldn't come off. "That's too hard," she said. "Just go ahead and put it in me." But there was nothing doing down there. He stroked himself. "Do that in the bathroom," Cindy said. "I can hear it slapping around. It's disgusting." When he got up, she grabbed the sheets and pulled them over her. He ran the water until the bath was full and eased himself into the tub. He couldn't remember the last time he took a bath. It was so relaxing he woke up a few hours later, shivering, barely able to make it to the bed.

"This sort of thing happens to older men," Cindy says, looking down at her magazine. "It has to do with stress and failure and a lack of reckoning with your past. Here, it's all right here."

She hands Leonard a folded-over magazine and points at an article with a photograph of a man looking lost and confused, sitting on a pointy rock, staring at the sparkling blue ocean.

TROUBLE IN BED = TROUBLE IN HEAD

BY FRIEDA CALLOWAY

. . . As we know, men are easily embarrassed by sex. It's something that stems from childhood, giggling at boobs and butts while covering their stiffening crotches. But with age and experience, especially in this country, comes a period of malaise that can lead to impotence.

Tell me if you've heard these excuses before:

"I've had a long day."

"I must've eaten something funky at lunch."

"My back is stiff."

"You don't seem into it."

Women remember the bra-snapping, dress-lifting, fellatio-mimicking boy in the back of the classroom. We didn't like him then, but we wonder, Where is he now? That horniness comes in handy when you yourself have had a long day.

At first we feel anger, then a period of inadequacy, followed by apathy. You've considered an affair with your kids' soccer coach, but, believe me, he's no different. The real issue isn't . . .

Wait, Frieda the Virginity Collector? He turns the page. At the bottom is a photograph of her in a tree pose on the beach. It *is* Frieda. She had been a senior at Wequaquet High when Leonard was a freshman. She was known for taking boys' virginities. It was like a hobby for her. A year before he started going with Cindy, Leonard lay stiff as a mummy on Frieda's bed as she rolled her hips over him until he burst. Afterward she thanked him and kissed his cheek.

According to the magazine, she's a *freelance writer, life coach, and certified yoga instructor, currently living in Boynton Beach, Florida.*

Leonard pretends to keep reading, looking at her photograph, thinking maybe this is a sign.

LEONARD TEACHES American history at Wequaquet High. Most of what he teaches is washed away in the sludge of microwavable foods, pink music, and reality-television shows. You can't scream in the sludge, he tells his students, they won't hear you. But still they bark in the hallways, shouting, "Imf imf imf!"

It's difficult to get time alone. Sometimes he hides in the janitor's closet to catch his breath. If he's in there too long, he gets high on the ammonia and stumbles out dizzy. This makes for an interesting lecture on the American Revolution.

Home is no solace. Not a room in the house he can call his own; each one a box of toys, foul smells, and bad drawings.

At night, Cindy holds her tablet on her knees, the screen so bright it swells out into his field of vision, making it difficult to read from *Confederate Love Songs,* the book she had given to their children to give to Leonard for his birthday:

> "I have f h in what we're doing, but can I re y on faith
> a ne?"

Cindy taps the screen, it goes dark; taps again, and it shines like a spotlight. Finally she pulls the cover over the screen, shuffles to the bathroom, pees with the door open, flicks shreds of dinner out of her teeth with floss, gargles like a woman drowning, shakes her contacts clean, gets back into bed, and stretches her arms above her head and draws her knees up as if falling from a cliff into a deep blue lake. She says good night in a tone suited for a doorman and, minutes later, asks Leonard to shut the light off or read downstairs. She's got a busy day tomorrow. The tablet will remind them what's next, with a five-second symphony of electronic noise. The past is reduced to useful mistakes: overpriced restaurants, distrustful mechanics, people they shouldn't invite to the kids' next birthday parties, because they didn't bring a gift and ate more than anyone else.

The couch, the quiet, the place that is not this place is instead more horrific. Appreciate what you have, Leonard. Don't be so morose.

> . . . My dear Mary-Alice, I saw a man take a ball to the
> leg during our last battle. They poured whiskey on the

wound and whiskey down his throat. He was given a rotted tree branch to bite down on while they sawed the leg off at the knee. His teeth broke through the branch, broke through his tongue. There's no indication he's to be sent home. He is valuable in that he is a broad man with a wide back and we can stack many supplies on top of him . . .

Leonard tries to relax. He meditates, medicates, and masturbates. Some nights he doesn't sleep. Some nights he thinks about his mother. He wonders if she's looking down at him, at the awkward man she produced, gripping his penis and making uncomfortable-looking faces as he comes. His mother had been a hopeless woman. She always talked about death—death of her parents, of people in town she knew, of people she had read about in the paper, and, most of all, her own death.

She had said, "I'm going to die, Leonard. Me."

TWO DAYS later, Leonard decides to take a week off from school. He tells Cindy that he's flying to Virginia for the annual National Council of History Education conference. Cindy says time away will be good for the both of them. She cares, but maybe she cares too much. As a part-time hairstylist at Uppercuts, she's always trying to make the customers feel better. She tells balding men they're sexy, overweight women that the hair is what men really care about, kids with impossible cowlicks to feel fortunate they're not bald or fat.

"I'll miss you," Leonard says.

Cindy touches her nose. Her sign for *ditto*.

* * *

AT THE West Palm Beach airport, Leonard rents a car and drives along the coastline to the Marriott. He walks confidently through the doors with his carry-on and greets the girl at the front desk, who's standing in front of a giant aquarium filled with fluorescent fish. He asks her if she's in school. She's not. She says she's as smart as she needs to be. She asks where he's from.

"Imagine the complete opposite of here," he says.

Showered, unwound, dressed in jeans and a green V-neck T-shirt, hair combed and messed like in a casual-it-just-happened-while-I-was-out kind of way, he turns side to side in the mirror. Only problem is his whiteness, too white for Florida.

Every block has a strip mall with a tanning salon, a yoga studio, and a smoothie place. And everyone looks fit, as though they've never had to start from scratch. To be like them, Roman-esque, resurrected beings of a past civilization that had no cars, no soft drinks, no Taco Bells. In the Valhalla Palms strip mall, where Frieda's studio is, Leonard decides to stop into a place called Tan-Talizing. He pays for a half-hour cyber-dome special, steps up into the pod and lies flat, with the blue light descending on his nearly naked body. Hypnotic music plays.

What to say? Frieda, is that you? . . . Frieda? I can't believe this. I was in Florida for a conference and saw your card at the tanning . . . Frieda? It's Leonard. Do you remember me? I guess you could say I've changed over the years. Who hasn't? Right, who hasn't?

Pod door rises. The hairs on his body tingle.

"Three more sessions and you should be brown as cara-mel," the overly peppy woman behind the counter says.

Two doors down is the Healing Zone. Leonard enters the lobby and stands at the glacier-glass door into the main room, rolling his neck. He pulls the door handle, then pushes, and then pulls again. There's a note on the bulletin board to his right: *If you happen to be late, take a seat and meditate.* Lucky for him, unlucky for the plus-size woman covering her bottom with crossed hands, the door opens and he inches his way into the foul-smelling, dimly lit studio.

There's Frieda up front, her back arched, the same plump breasts and flat stomach and strong legs. He remembers how her body was smooth and shaved. He could've spent hours down there. He should've spent hours down there, listening to her moan.

"Now exhale," she says, and lowers down. "Feel the air leaving your stomach, rising up through your chest, emptying from your mouth; feel the pressure release from your fingertips, your hands, your arms, your neck. Lie still as a corpse; relieve yourself of all thoughts; there is no past and no future, there is no you or I or we, there is only the eternal being, the ever-present spirit—"

An old man in a purple sweatsuit sits up and shouts, "Miss! How'm I supposed to relax with you talking all this nonsense the whole time?"

"Most people find it relaxing to listen," Frieda says in an even, deferential tone.

"I'm not so sure about that, miss. I think we need to take a vote. We still live in a democracy, don't we, despite all the evidence?"

A woman, presumably the man's wife, smacks his hand and says, "Harold, let her do her business."

"We've already had one woman do her business in here tonight," Harold mutters.

"Now, breathe in," Frieda continues. "Feel the air enter and fill your body, feel your body expand, listen to your heart pumping, feel the blood run through your veins, hold the air inside you, and then exhale slowly . . . slowly . . . releasing . . ."

Harold is shaking his head, or maybe it's a tremor.

"When do we get to the sexy stuff?" he shouts.

"Harold!"

"We have to loosen everything up first, Mr. Hart," Frieda says, "or else we might displace something very important to us."

As the class continues to breathe, Frieda stands up and follows a path of bare floor between colored mats and sagging, wheezing bodies.

"Is that Leonard Putter?" she says, smiling, those plump lips and the curved tip of her nose and that thick blond hair bouncing about her neck.

"I'm in town for a . . . thing. . . . Stopped to get some lunch . . . Saw your name on the—"

"You've been reading me, haven't you?" she says confidently, hands at her hips, tight black form-fitting yoga pants showcasing her firm thighs.

"My wife showed me an article, but that's not—"

"How is Cindy?"

"She's good. She's sort of okay."

"Oh."

"The thing is . . ."

"This is a purposeful visit, isn't it? This is supposed to change your life."

"I'm not predicting anything."

"I thought I'd see you again. I just didn't know in what form."

"Form?"

"I'm joking. Don't think I'm a wack job just because I'm into spiritual fitness."

"Right. Sorry. I'm nervous. You don't look much older than you did in high school."

"Bull crap. But thank you."

"I mean, I'm having problems back home."

"Leonard." She begins fixing his hair, fanning it across his forehead, a moment of intimacy between old lovers, perhaps. "You're welcome to sit in," she says, and heads back to her mat. "Now it's time to practice our Kegel exercises," she says to the class. "Don't clench, pull. We're getting closer to that sexy stuff, Mr. Hart."

Leonard tries to follow along with the class, clenching his member.

After a short break, Frieda calls him to join her on the mat. She wraps her legs around his waist and instructs the women in the class to do the same.

"Now pull yourself up onto your partner's lap," she says. "You can use your hands if you have to."

Frieda has spider-like legs; her breasts push up against Leonard's chin.

"Just like old times," she whispers. Then to the class, "You should feel your partner growing warm beneath you. Take in this energy, hold it inside you, let it fill you up, let it nourish you; stretch your arms into the air, breathe; you are a tree, growing from that pulsing warmth beneath you; grow, grow, grow."

At this point Leonard's hard as a rock, but Frieda doesn't seem to notice or doesn't care. She's growing. Her breasts hang in front of his face. He remembers those brown-button nipples brushing across his lips.

From the back of the room, Harold Hart shouts, "That's the ticket!"

AFTER CLASS, they sit on stools at the juice bar and catch up.

"What do you do for work these days?" she asks.

"I teach history at Wequaquet High."

"Oh, right, I think I remember hearing that. I must've forgotten because it's so depressing to think of someone you love living in such a helpless environment."

"Did you say you love me?"

"Of course. I love everyone who's been inside my body. How could I not?"

"I never looked at it that way. Does it work the other way, too?"

"It should," Frieda says, and takes a sip of her kale juice.

"I'll be honest. I've been having trouble in bed. I can't make it work. I don't know if it's Cindy or me or what, but being here and seeing you and thinking about us on your parents' couch while they were passed out drunk, fiddling around inside each other's jeans, it's getting me hard."

"See? What irony. It's your own history you've forgotten, and you teach history, for crying out loud! I remember you had such a hard, handsome dick. Not too big, not too small."

"Why do you think it won't respond anymore?"

"Maybe it's bored. Sometimes couples get into this routine where they have sex in the same place, in the same position, with the same beginning and ending, and their privates just get tired of it. They go to sleep and dream of new adventures. You have to remember that pricks and pussies have fantasies, too."

"Like separate beings?"

"I think so. And trust me when I tell you, you're not the only one who has had issues down there. Hitler once had a woman shot when he couldn't get it up. He was a syphilitic bisexual who had to find other ways to get off, so he ordered young girls to squat over him and urinate or defecate on his chest, whichever came first, preferably both."

"I knew I had something in common with Hitler."

Frieda finishes her smoothie and lets out an emphatic "Ah!"

"Have you ever made love during a tropical storm?" she asks.

"No. This is my first time in Florida. Well, except when my parents took me to Disney World for my sixth birthday and it rained the whole time we were there, and at breakfast one morning Goofy pinched my ear so hard it turned red and my father ended up spending half our vacation trying to find the specific Disney authority that handled the firing of Goofy, which there was obviously more than one, and you couldn't really do a lineup, and he kept asking me, after finally tracking down the right official and filing his complaint, 'Do you remember what color pants the Goofy that hurt you was wearing?' That's the only way they can tell the difference. Each one wears different-color pants. And I couldn't remember, so then my father was angrier with my lack of being able to remember than with the Goofy that hurt me, and eventually we left a day earlier than planned."

"Forget your Disney vacation. When the wind and rain start beating against the windowpanes, you can feel the vibration all through your body. It's like some force enters you, and it takes sex to a whole other level."

Leonard wishes the wind would pick up and the ocean would swell and the rain would start pouring down.

"I want to stay faithful to Cindy."

"You're a prideful man," Frieda says. "Even when you were fifteen, you were full of pride. I guess the question you need to ask yourself now is how far has that pride taken you in life?"

★   ★   ★

BACK IN his room at the Marriott, exhausted, lonely, weak, Leonard orders a cheeseburger from room service. Big table, white linen, small ketchup bottle, a haphazard *voilà* given by the Cuban waiter, a burger the size of his palm, a bun twice the size of the burger, French fries undercooked, the cap on his ginger ale impossible to pop off.

The bill is twenty-two dollars, including gratuity.

An hour later, the burger isn't sitting well. There's a rumbling in his stomach. He makes tea and lies down with *Confederate Love Songs*:

We are in camp, not far from Chattanooga. I am tired and my clothes are streaked with blood. I saw a man this morning on my walk to get firewood. He had been slaughtered two maybe three days ago, it seemed. There were maggots crawling from his nostrils. But that did not trouble me, as I have seen it in this war, for there are so many bodies it is impossible to dispose of all of them in a timely fashion. No. What I saw is unspeakable, almost too difficult to write. But I am alone and I trust you will understand that I cannot sit with these images and still fight this war with a competent state of mind. The body was stripped, everything but the man's socks, which were full of holes, and at the groin there was only a stump, and I thought it good that he was dead. Sylvia, I know you will be troubled by this, but who else can I confide in besides you after God knows now what I have seen? It might not matter, as I cannot be sure the man I will give this letter to will follow through with his promise, which he has given to many men since his discharge. It is very possible he

will be slain, his horse, too, and the letters will be burnt
with the man and horse.

THE PHONE rings.

Frieda says, "I've been thinking . . . the Marriott is overpriced, and I've heard they got bugs. So you'll stay the night at
my place."

"That's kind of you, but I don't—"

"Oh, please. I'm in the lobby. I've already checked you out."

THEY WALK up a rise and over wooden planks to a little yellow
bungalow with a Mayan sundial hanging beside the sliding
door. On the lounge chair is a naked man tapping a pencil
against his head. His body is shaved—pink and venous, like the
underside of a tongue. His penis is a small bulb of light. He's
reading *Your Five-Year Plan,* making notes in the margins. Frieda
doesn't make a proper introduction. She says, "That's Brian. He
rents a room. Despite the nudity, he's a perfect tenant." They
sit on the steps of the deck and listen to the ocean dispense its
collections.

"So," Frieda says plainly, "big picture."

Leonard tells her he's concerned about his marriage. He
can't remember what it was like to love Cindy, to be in love.

"It's still inside you," she says, rubbing his back. "You have
to pull it out, fight against forgetting, or you'll end up lonely
and freakish."

Brian gets up and strolls past them, his penis hanging like a
chili pepper. He stops and scratches the back of his head.

"Frieda," he says. "Year three is impossible to figure out.
After all, what will I do with that money? I've never wanted

anything, but the money will make me start wanting things. Or do I give it to a charity? And then, I think, will I even be here? Maybe I'll go back home and take care of my folks. Maybe I'll move to Barcelona. So many people say Barcelona is the most beautiful city on earth. How would I know? Maybe it's not. Maybe it's Saskatoon." He looks down at his book. "I'm going to make stuffed peppers," he says. "I'll make extra for you and your friend."

ON THE beach, they are like kids again, jumping, running, diving, splashing, and howling. The waves bound under the glowing face of the moon. They share a bottle of wine. The wind dries them off. They walk into the house, past Brian, who is staring at a recipe book, still naked, very close to the lit stovetop. Frieda hands Leonard a towel. They sit on the edge of her bed. She strokes the inside of his leg, then puts her hand under his shirt and curls his chest hair in her fingers. She kisses his neck and the spot just behind his earlobe.

"Fuck me," she whispers.

"What?"

"Jesus, how long has it been?"

"Sorry, oh . . . you want me to fuck you?"

"I doubt you remember the little mole near my vagina, or the scar along my rib cage from when I tried to sneak back into my house through the doggy door."

"No. Yes. You were in the hospital. My mother brought me to see you. I gave you a chocolate orange."

"Uh-huh. And do you remember where I was most ticklish?"

"Your armpits?"

"Now that's where I like to be kissed and licked. What about Cindy—where is she most ticklish?"

"Her feet."

"Have you ever sucked on her toes or licked the bottoms of her feet?"

"No."

"These places where we laugh when touched, we moan when kissed."

Frieda stretches her arms over her head, creates a bow—unshaven, smell of salt and some animal scent Leonard can't quite identify. He needles his tongue through the soft hairs. She shivers. Her moans are like gasps. Each time she rocks forward, she checks his temple with her elbow. Finally, she lowers her arms and puts her hands on his shoulders.

"Should we turn the lights off?" he asks her.

"Darkness poisons a good fuck," she says.

That kind of language, Leonard thinks. I miss saying it out loud.

"Lights on, then?" he says.

She leans back and spreads her legs wide.

"Look at my vagina," she says. "Tell me what you see."

He's on his stomach, examining the opening.

"I don't know what to say."

"Your view is different than mine. It will always be different. I have one hundred and thirty-six versions of my pussy. Don't you understand?"

"Well, it's . . . it's sort of like a little house, I guess you could say, with a cupola on the roof here."

"Oh, mmm . . . keep your finger . . . yes, rub that, what did you call it? A cupola?"

"If you hadn't put me on the spot—oh, there's the mole. I remember now."

"I spy. That's what you used to say. Now put your cock in me and hold still."

Slowly, she pulls him farther inside her, as though ingesting this part of him that now seems separate from his body, without defense against the jungle: its reptiles, insects, and animals, and the sweet, beautiful flowers they hide behind. The farther he's drawn in, the firmer he gets. She arches her back, squeezes him at the base until he can no longer feel himself. He watches her as a boy watches an old mystic woman at the far end of a carnival, her hair wild, eyes rolling back, veins stretching in her neck, until finally he's released, dripping at the head. She falls back onto the sheets, her body shuddering in little spasmodic bursts.

"Is there some way I can . . . repay you?" Leonard asks.

Frieda laughs.

"I'm not a hooker," she says.

"Right, sorry. I think I need some air."

"Bring me back a stuffed pepper," she says. "I'm starving."

BRIAN IS outside on the porch, drinking a beer. Leonard sits down beside him. In the dark, he can see Brian's protruding shoulder blades, like wings trying to emerge from his skin.

"It's peaceful here," Leonard says.

"Too peaceful," Brian says. "Set for a riot if you ask me. Did you try the peppers?"

"Not yet."

"You know what the most popular food in prison is?"

"What's that?"

"Honey buns."

"Really?"

"Really. Do you know how many calories are in one honey bun?"

"How many?"

"Four hundred and forty calories. Two hundred and twenty-five of those are from fat, mainly saturated fat. But do you know why they're so popular?"

"Because they're cheap?"

"No, no, no. The reason they're so popular"—Brian finishes the bottle, jabs his chest with his fist—"the reason they're so popular is because they remind the inmates of home. That's how powerful something like a honey bun can be. It can bring back memories. This fat hunk of sugared dough has the capacity to resurrect a place and time. You've never seen so many full-grown men with glazed lips, laughing, telling stories, acknowledging you as a brother in their honey-bun community. It's a really beautiful thing."

LEONARD PLACES two stuffed peppers on a napkin and brings them to Frieda in the bedroom.

"Your friend is a little strange," he says, handing them to her.

"He's had a rough go of it. I swear he could get caught stealing a pack of chewing gum."

"Is he . . . you know . . . on the run?"

"He's a friend of a friend. I don't know his story, haven't asked. He's a magician in the kitchen and pays his rent on time."

"And his being naked doesn't bother you?"

"I understand it. If you've always been one way and it's never worked out for you, then it makes sense to try the opposite."

They eat the stuffed peppers, silent, munching.

"These are delicious," Leonard says.

Frieda sits back against the headboard. Her hair is sprung from her head, face flushed from the heat of the pepper.

"Sometimes I think about home," she says. "But I think about it the way it was when I was young, when everything was big and it took a lot of work to get from one place to the next. Last time I was back there, everything seemed so small, as though the houses had all shrunk. I'd heard about Donna's kid being killed, and I drove by her old house, but it was the house she grew up in and there were other people living there, and I was thinking about how Donna and I used to sneak out together and smoke cigarettes near the lake and talk for hours about what we were going to do with our lives, how we were going to travel and meet interesting men and be rich—you know, stupid dreams. At home, I could barely move around in my old room. My mother called me to dinner and I felt this incredible stabbing in my chest. I actually had to go to the hospital. They said I had generalized anxiety disorder. GAD, they called it. 'She's GAD,' I heard the doctor tell the nurse. I kept repeating it in my head. I'm GAD or I'm a GAD. Anyway, they gave me some pills. I threw them out. I don't think I'll be going back home anytime soon."

"Maybe I should think about moving here."

"Oh, Leonard, this is not the place for you."

"Why not?"

"It's just that . . . you're attracted to what's new, but what seems strange at first becomes normal, becomes reality, and then what will you have? You'll get lost. You won't *mean* anything."

The idea of meaning something takes a second to sink in. What do I mean to my students, Leonard thinks, to my friends, my kids, Cindy? They depend on me, don't they? They need me, don't they?

"Time for bed," Frieda says, sinking beneath the covers. "Could you get the lights, please?"

★   ★   ★

LEONARD CAN'T sleep. Frieda lies beside him, snoring. The kitchen is a mess: empty wine bottles, dirty dishes, black smudges dried on the baking sheet, now sticking out of the sink like a boat going down. He misses Cindy. He misses their house and how it smells. He misses her soft touch on the back of his neck as he does the dishes after dinner, her asking if he'll read to the kids, if he can remember to pick up this or that tomorrow, if he'll move some savings into the checking account so she can repaint the bedroom. Simple things, a life, mysterious and strange when your son says he saw a bear roaming in the backyard and your daughter tosses everything from the fridge into a giant bowl and mixes it with a wooden spoon and serves it for dessert. Yes, he already misses that.

He drives to the airport, checks in.

"Your plane doesn't leave for another five hours," the lady at the counter says.

"I have a book."

Leonard takes a seat on a cracked leather chair looking out at the tarmac and opens *Confederate Love Songs*:

> Dear Eleanor, I can say now for certain I will be coming home. By what means and course, I do not know. I am not sure where we are, though a fellow soldier has said we are not far from Virginia. He can tell by the air and the shape of the sky and the foul smell of dogwood trees. I do not know if you are alive or if the children are safe or what has happened since I left Franklin. It is green here, very green, and there are lightning bugs. The other night I caught one and felt it fluttering in my cupped hands, and I thought of you and Maggie and William and little Jacob. I wept, and while I wept I prayed and forgot about the bug, until I finished pray-

ing and saw that it was crushed into the lifeline of my
palm. . . .

The book slips from his hands. Of course, he thinks, dozing off,
what does Rome know of rat and lizard? The rats and the lizards, what do they know of each other?

He feels a tap on his shoulder and looks up at a cute, petite
flight attendant.

"Sir, is this your plane?"

Leonard nods.

"We're leaving now," she says. "Everyone's waiting for you."

LOST DOG

~~~~~

THERE ARE TIMES when absolutely nothing is happening. That's when you know something's about to happen. You hear F-17s flying overhead, the sound like tearing paper. Then the missiles and the crushing force of wind and all of us grabbing our gear and jumping into the Humvees, barreling toward the smoke in the distance. No one looks scared. Sure, guys are puking out the windows, but that's on account of the heat. Some of it splashes on the windshield. Our squad leader issues the coordinates. Everything looks the same. We pass the same palm tree over and over, as if we're going through a time warp that takes us five minutes back every five minutes. Then we're in a village—what used to be a village. You've never heard women cry like these women here. It comes gushing out of their bodies. We have to keep them at a distance even though they look like they want to be held. I've seen them explode.

"I miss my kid," Owen says. "She lost her first tooth a few

days ago. It came loose when she was eating pizza and she didn't realize it and ended up swallowing it. There was nothing to put under her pillow, but Julie gave her a five-dollar bill, anyway. Now she knows for sure there isn't a tooth fairy, because the tooth fairy doesn't pay for nothing."

The air is full of dust. We're not destroyers; we go through what's been destroyed. I see a Haji's arm stuck like a small flag in the sand, the first three fingers blown off. There's an infantry watch around his wrist, still ticking. "This wouldn't be such a bad advertisement for the manufacturer," Owen says. He picks up the arm and it flies out of his hand. "Fuck, it's burning." We look at it, up ahead in a divot in the sand. Maybe it'll move again. I once saw a movie about a killer hand. It could be they got the idea from something like this. Then a Humvee rolls over the arm and it sticks in the treads, waving back at us for a brief moment before the wheel cuts a furrow through the wreckage.

OWEN SAYS he hasn't taken a shit in three weeks. It's the camel spiders, he says. "I'm afraid they're going to bite my nuts." I tell him to get a bucket. He says it doesn't matter. At mess, we eat chicken livers and onions, mashed potatoes and broccoli. Someone feeling sorry for us sent over three giant boxes crammed with supermarket cupcakes. They're dry as hell, and most of us just eat the frosting.

SOME NIGHTS I lie awake and listen to them talk in their sleep. Owen has sex dreams. He raises his arms and grabs at the air and says, "Let me touch those big round titties." Tate always shouts the same thing: "It was me! I'm the one who did it!" The other night, Miller gave a fairly coherent sermon on right and wrong. The story had something to do with a boy whose friend had stolen some candy, and if the boy told, he'd lose the friend, but if he didn't, he'd go to hell. When Miller was through, he began to snore. I looked over and saw that a few of the other guys had been listening, too. So as Miller slept on, we shaved his legs. Next morning we whistled at him in the shower.

NO ONE touches us. You realize this about three months in, during a moment of quiet. You realize that all your life you've been touched by people: parents, grandparents, brothers, sisters, girlfriends, wives. You knock elbows with a stranger in a movie theater, shake hands with a friend of a friend, dance in a bar with a woman you just met.

A group of cheerleaders flew over here a couple of months back, and some of the guys got to hug them and get their pictures taken with the girls on their laps. The cheerleaders smiled and giggled and waved and cheered. I only got close enough to smell them. They smelled like peppermints.

When they left, the guys were sad as hell. They burned the photographs. One guy named Silver went out and shot three cats and brought them back and buried them. He was analyzed and discharged. While he packed his stuff, a bunch of us gave him a hard time. He didn't say anything. Right before he left, he pulled me aside and told me to take care of those cats.

"They don't have anyone to look after them," he said. "And you can't trust these jerk-offs to look after themselves, let alone a harmless animal."

I doubt he remembers any of this. I hear they put so much stuff in you.

SOMETIMES IT'S boring out here. You never know when you're about to be sent into the night, so you never really sleep. Owen knows a guy who sells opium in small black pads the size of a thumbprint. He's real polite, Owen says. He knows how capitalism works. He knows we're not over here promoting American democracy but American business. He's willing to learn, get ahead of the game.

We break up the opium and roll it with tobacco. We get high but stay alert. It's a mysterious drug. I can see why people fall in love. When we're high, the desert is a peaceful place. We hang out and shoot the shit and it's like any other place that's ever been.

Later we go over to the trailer and watch Ultimate Fighting.

"This is what I'm going to do when I get back," Tate says.

He's got a book on judo and another on Brazilian jujitsu. They're both old and water-stained. Certain sentences are underlined in blue ink. One reads: *A wise opponent will transition to a choking technique.*

"What the hell are you guys on?" Tate says.

Owen is sitting in front of the television screen, softly whispering, "Boom, pow, zap." I'm holding the jujitsu book upside down and craning my neck to read it.

Tate flicks Owen's ear. Owen lunges dazedly for Tate but misses and crashes through the coffee table. Tate pins Owen's arms back and presses his neck forward. Owen's face is blue. This is a wise time to transition to a choking technique.

* * *

SOME OF the guys are glad to be here. Usually it's a girl back home. Things weren't working out. Or it's no money and two kids, or a wife with fat ankles and a fat ass. "I'd rather be killed," Miller says. We tell our pasts like horror stories.

SO IT gets depressing and we let go, turn to our guns and ammo, clean, check, and recheck. We play cards, wait, watch DVDs that constantly skip, rip them out and fling them across the room, wait, jerk off, sleep ten, twenty minutes at a time.

When we're out on patrol, I think about my girlfriend, Kiki. She's blond and big—five feet ten inches, not a scratch on her. I think about her legs; I wrap them around my waist, squeeze them tight, bury my face between them.

"You got a good one, Baker," Owen says.

"Me, I fit all the old ones together and make something perfect," Miller says.

"I haven't been able to jerk off in this place," Tate says.

"Camel spiders?" Owen says.

"What?" Tate scratches under his helmet, pulls off the strap, keeps scratching until there's blood in his fingernails.

"Think about how in, like, fifty years scientists will be able to design a woman to look just the way you want her to," Miller says.

"What good'll that do you when your nut bag's hanging around your ankles?" Tate says.

"Maybe they'll fix that, too."

FOLLOWING WEEK, Miller steps on an IED and his right leg's blown off at the thigh. He's knocked out, but there must be a pulse, because Owen's giving him CPR. Problem is, blood's shooting out the opening with each pump to his chest. Finally, Tate smacks the back of Owen's head, stuffs the leg with Quik-Clot, and ties a bandage above the wound. Medics arrive. A chopper. So mouths are moving but no one can hear what anyone's saying. I'm saying, "We need to get the fuck out of here."

That night, Tate and Owen play horseshoes until dawn. I try to sleep, but I keep seeing particles of Miller's leg floating around me like dust. As they stumble into bed, Owen lets an iron fly right past Tate's face. Tate gets up and punches him in the neck. Owen staggers back and gasps for breath.

"Don't fight it," Tate says.

Owen collapses onto his bed, still gasping.

Anytime I got hurt when I was a kid, my mother would sing to me. She had a terrible voice. I never told her that, because it made her feel better to think she was making me feel better.

What I think I mean is that as long as we're not alone, it's not so bad.

THE WAR has to end at some point. At least that's the thought. Or maybe thinking that makes it easier to be so out of line.

Just before night patrol, Tate fills a cup with arrack and pours water in it so that it looks like milk. "Nightcap," he says, and he takes a gulp and bats the sides of his head with his fists. He passes it to Owen, then to me. I don't drink the stuff, because it makes my stomach burn, and because someone's got to drive.

We're trailing three HVs; radios murmur; Tate lets out a sickly belch.

No fire yet. Nothing yet. So it's waiting for us. You can only refer to it as *it*, the thing that tries to kill you.

A while passes, you get into this daze; this daze gets you into trouble. I haven't noticed that our BFTs are down and the HVs ahead are out of sight. What I see up ahead is a dog. Black ears, black snout, big paws, ribs shoving through a narrow torso, sloped head, eyes stretched back almost to the sides of his face.

"What kind of dog is that?" I ask.

"Fucking beast," Tate says.

"He looks scared."

"That's how he pulls you in."

Owen steps out, flashes a light on the ground. He's worried about the spiders. The dog doesn't bark, doesn't whine. As Owen approaches, the dog lies down and rolls onto his back. Owen rubs the dog's stomach, and his legs wave in the air. Tate and I get out and move toward them. So much shit attached to us it's difficult to squat down. But there's nothing moving out here except the wind and the sand. I take off my pack and my rifle, unhook my vest, open an MRE, let the dog eat.

"I wish I were a dog," Owen says. "Short life, no responsibilities, always getting petted."

"Shut the fuck up," Tate says.

But then the dog is licking Tate's palm. "Oh, Jesus," he says, and he rolls over and the dog puts his paws on Tate's chest and licks his face and ears and Tate laughs and says, "No, stop it, no," but in a way that makes it clear he doesn't really want it to stop, he wants it to go on forever.

Then Tate's gun fires and the dog darts into the night.

"You fucking idiot," Owen says. "Now they'll know we're here."

"The fucking spiders?" Tate turns his light on the empty desert, on a whirl of dust rushing nowhere. "We've got to find him," he says.

"Find who?" Owen says.

"That dog. He's all alone."

"You're out of your mind."

"What's that?" Tate levels the gun at Owen.

"You don't scare me, pal."

"Let's vote on it, then," Tate says democratically, and he flicks his eyes to me.

Crazy has my support, 100 percent. "I think the dog deserves better," I say.

"That liquor's got you high," Owen says.

"I didn't drink any of it."

"Maybe you should have; maybe you'd see things more clearly."

"The longer we stand around here arguing," Tate says, "the farther away he gets."

THE HUMVEE'S motor echoes like we're driving in a cave. Owen keeps smacking the BFT panel. We see palm tree, palm tree, three-foot stone wall (check for Haji; knock it down), palm tree. Then an abandoned car with no windshield. We stop the Humvee and walk toward it slowly. The paint is peeled off, console torn out, dog feces in the backseat.

"This must be where he sleeps," Tate says.

He checks underneath the car, turning the light back and forth, and finds a score of camel spiders.

Owen freaks, jumps to the hood and then the roof, leaving a dent that pops up with a bang. Tate whips out his gun and fires into the dark.

"What the hell's the matter with you?" I say.

Tate snaps the dust off his uniform. "Let's clear out."

"I'm not going anywhere," Owen says. "I counted thirty-three of those big bastards."

"Don't be such a fucking baby. We can't stay here. We can't

let that dog just wander around with these spiders every-where."

"They're everywhere?" Owen says. "I counted thirty-three."

"Can you make it back to the Humvee?" I ask Owen.

"We're not taking the Humvee," Tate says. "We're not going to find the dog in the Humvee."

"So what are we going to do?" I nod my head at Owen, speak quietly: "I think he's not well."

"Then it's you and me, Baker. We're pretty well fucked either way."

Tate turns and walks into the night.

I follow. When I look back for Owen, I can only make out his light, scanning the ground.

Tate shouts, "Those spiders won't stay grounded for long."

WE WALK for what feels like miles.

The dark sky opens up with a thick burst of ash. "I smell fresh piss," Tate says.

"The sun'll be up in an hour or so. Then what?"

"Then we'll be able to see better."

"I'm worried about Owen."

"Owen's fine. I don't even remember if I saw any spiders or not."

"I saw them."

"Maybe you did, maybe you didn't. It's all in the past now."

SOME SORT of village, I guess you'd call it. Square mud huts form an *L*, and a rusted old truck with slats of wood fencing framing the bed sits in the center like a piece of modern art. A few kids are kicking a soccer ball back and forth, and when they see us, they stop and stare. One of them picks his nose and puts his finger in his mouth. Behind the truck is a group of Hajis, some squatting, some standing, one squeezing the back of a dog's neck. Our dog.

I know *hi* and *bye, yes* and *no,* but that's about it. There's no time to study. So I let Tate take over, and he screams something that means nothing to them at first but over time comes to mean lying facedown in the dirt with a gun pointed at them. And then it can never mean anything else.

Only the guy with the dog doesn't seem to understand, and Tate walks toward him, keeping the gun aimed at his head until the only thing separating them is the gun. The man whimpers; tears push out from his eyes. Finally, his knees buckle and he's on the ground, prostrate, his hands clasped behind his bowed head.

The other men haven't moved. They're like dummies in a shop window.

The dog looks up at Tate, and Tate smiles and lowers his hand, and the dog turns suddenly and scampers into one of the huts.

"Okay, okay," Tate says, and I can tell something terrible is about to happen, like an instinct; some terrible thing has been traveling through all of time to find its place, right here.

The dog barks. Mournfully, Tate looks for him. The men laugh. I scan the huts. The dog is now at the entrance to one, beside a large, cloaked woman. She bends down and pets the dog. Then she slices his throat.

"Oh, Jesus," I shout.

Tate lets out a sound of pure anguish and grabs the man by the collar, lifting him right off his feet. The other men are up and yelling now.

"Shut up!" I cry. "Please, just shut the hell up!"

But they don't understand. I have to fire my rifle in the air.

Still, they keep going. I have to fire at their feet. Finally they scatter.

"I've lost them," I say. "We need to get out of here."

There's no response. I glance around. There's no sign of Tate.

I walk slowly toward the hut, past the dog, blood still draining from his neck, mouth open, teeth chipped. He lets out a cough, just a reflex. When I was a kid we had to put down our Boston terrier, Pickles. After the shot, his body quaked and all that energy left him in a gasp.

The man and his wife are on the floor with their hands behind their heads, mouthing voiceless prayers. Tate's in a fighting position, his right leg slightly behind his left, arms up, aiming his rifle. But he's aiming it above them, at the wall behind. I look in his eyes, and he doesn't seem wholly here.

"Tate?" I say.

He doesn't react.

"Is the rifle necessary?"

"They killed that poor dog," he says.

What to say in a moment like this? Tate's mouth hanging open; the husband and wife on their knees, praying.

I tell him I think the dog's going to make it.

"You lying son of a bitch," he says.

"There'll be other dogs," I say.

"But not that one," he says, pushing the muzzle of the gun against the woman's head. "That dog was perfect."

Quietly, I remove my pistol and train it on Tate. I haven't fired it since basic. It feels light in my hand.

"Put the gun down, Tate."

"It's not right," he says. "Someone's got to make it right." His fingers tighten on the forestock.

I aim the pistol at his calf, but when I fire, it jumps and I hit him in the flank. He's pushed forward by the force of the bullet and he falls on top of the woman, dropping his rifle. The man shoves him off, and the couple scrambles to their feet. They press their hands together and bow as they hurry outside. I pick up Tate's rifle.

He's moaning and cursing, kicking his legs.

"I'm sorry, man. I didn't have a choice."

"You didn't have to put a fucking bullet in me."

I take off his jacket and realize he's not wearing a vest. I apply pressure to the wound. The blood is gushing out between my fingers.

"How'm I gonna get out of here?"

"I'll carry you."

I drape his arm over my shoulder and help him to his feet.

The men from before are gathered around the truck, laughing. The kids, too. One of them mimics being shot and hops around with his hands pressed to his side.

In the shade of the truck, the dog lies in a crumpled heap, bleeding out.

I tell Tate not to pay attention to them, not to even look in their direction. They're harmless.

WHEN WE'RE out a little ways, I give Tate a morphine shot and tell him to keep his hand over the hole. It's hard work carrying both packs, the two rifles, and Tate, who can barely shuffle his feet, but I have to keep moving, I have to get him back. He says he's had a couple of toes blown off and his neck grazed, but never has he been plugged with a bullet.

I can't apologize enough.

"Does it hurt?"

"No, I don't feel anything, unless numb is a feeling. Is numb a feeling?"

"Can I tell you something?"

"Go on."

"You won't get mad?"

"What can I do?"

"I'm not sure where we're headed. I mean, I know we walked fairly straight from that car, but I can't be sure."

"You weren't paying attention?"

"I was following you. You were following the dog. Did we head east, maybe? Is it possible we headed east?"

Tate groans.

I tell him I'm sorry. I'm real sorry.

THE SUN never seems to move during the day. It stays right above wherever you are, cut flat, sucking all the energy from your body. I hold Tate on his feet and give him some water. He chokes it back. The wind picks up, and we're shrouded in dust. To our right is a set of tire tracks.

I ask Tate if he thinks Owen's all right.

"It's hard to give a simple answer to that question, knowing all the intricate actions that take place over a specific period of time."

"He could've been captured? Is that what you're saying?"

"Could've been. Or maybe the spiders got to him. Or maybe he ran back to the Humvee and got the BFT working, radioed for help. Or maybe he's asleep in that car. Maybe he was asleep in that car and the car exploded and he's alive but only for a little while longer. See what I mean?"

We follow the tracks until the wind picks up again and covers them over. I'm hungry and tired and carrying Tate's entire weight. I tell him I have to take a break.

"Didn't we pass a tree?" he says.

"I'm not sure."

"Is there even a tree out here, just one shitty, dying tree with a few shitty, dying palms for some shade? When you don't need a tree, you see a tree. But when you need one—"

"We still have your MRE, right?"

"Why? What happened to yours?"

I dig Tate's MRE from his pack and split it between us.

"Oh, right," he says sadly. "Poor thing. His last meal was some shitty beef stew."

"I think he enjoyed it."

"Look at us, Baker. We think we're enjoying this, too, but it's just because we're hungry. And then we get these melted Tootsie Rolls, impossible to eat, rip your teeth right out."

I tell him we should save some, just in case.

"One tree," he says. "Is that too much to ask?"

HOURS LATER, and still no tree. A few sips of water left. Except for a pack of Skittles, the MRE is long gone. It's getting cold. Night again, then day. No one knows our coordinates. Poor Owen is trapped by the spiders. We've walked close to twenty miles, maybe more. My watch broke. It feels like we're in a pit of sludge. What's the point of having a girl like Kiki if she can't have me? And my poor dad, sometimes he gets so lonely, and right now I understand how that feels, but there's no way to tell him. Does he know how special he is?

Then it rains. Not typical rain but a heavy onslaught that comes in waves, rolling through the sky. Tate sucks water from the folds in my jacket, then slips to the ground.

I touch his forehead.

"I love pizza," he says. "I love ice cream and football and horses and motorcycles and comic books and swimming pools and carnivals and big tits and Christmas and the moon . . . Oh, God . . . Oh, God, what else?"

Soon, Tate falls asleep.

The rain dies, and the dust hangs in the air like fog, and out of the dust runs a dog. He looks no different from the other one, maybe a little thinner.

I tap Tate on the head and say, "The dog's back, Tate. Look. He's back. He wasn't killed after all."

Tate's not waking up.

I check his pulse.

Tate's got no pulse.

The dog starts licking Tate's face. I smack him on the rear and he turns and growls at me.

"Go ahead, then," I say. "Lick his stupid face."

In the morning, it's me and the dog and Tate. My knees are swollen and I can't feel my arms. The abandoned car is full of spiders. Some are as big as my head. A few have been shot and their guts are splattered all over the upholstery. The dog won't go near the car. He's barking like mad. There's no sign of Owen, but I see boot prints on the ground. I follow them this way and that. There's no sign of the Humvee, either.

I drop Tate where we started.

The dog keeps trotting ahead and looking back, his tongue wagging.

"Don't worry," I say. "I'm right behind you."

ACKNOWLEDGMENTS

For their insight and inspiration: Aaron Fagan, George Saunders, Mary Gaitskill, Richard Ford, Neil Young, Mary Karr, Michael Burkard, Arthur Flowers, Lee K. Abbott, Christopher Kennedy, Russell Banks, and Denis Johnson;

For their hard work and dedication: Claire Anderson-Wheeler, Sarah Bowlin, Courtney Reed, Meakin Armstrong, Paul Morris, and Michael Ray;

For their love and support: Kevin, Max, Diane, Frank, Tara, Matt, Dad, Sylvia, and H.P.;

Lastly, to my mother for her creative spirit, which lives in all of my work,

Thank You.

ABOUT THE AUTHOR

~

Patrick Dacey holds an MFA from Syracuse University. He has taught English at several universities in the United States and Mexico and has worked as a reporter, a landscaper, a door-to-door salesman, and most recently on the overnight staff at a homeless shelter and detox center. His stories have been featured in *Zoetrope: All-Story*, *Guernica*, *Bomb* magazine, and *Salt Hill*, among other publications. Originally from Cape Cod, Massachusetts, he currently lives in Virginia.